Charles King

Captain Dreams and Other Stories

Charles King

Captain Dreams and Other Stories

ISBN/EAN: 9783337083328

Printed in Europe, USA, Canada, Australia, Japan

Cover: Foto ©Andreas Hilbeck / pixelio.de

More available books at **www.hansebooks.com**

CAPTAIN DREAMS

AND

OTHER STORIES

EDITED BY

CAPT. CHARLES KING

PHILADELPHIA

J. B. LIPPINCOTT COMPANY

1895

PREFACE.

Encouraged by the success attending their
venture of a year gone by—their " Initial Experience" in a book of short stories from soldier
hands—the publishers again offer to the reading
public a little volume of similar matter. In
this day and generation, when military dramas
of every description are welcomed by the applause of eager and enthusiastic audiences, it
would seem as though an increasing demand
had sprung up for tales of military life, and
none are more popular than those which deal
with our own Blue Coats upon the Border,—
the guardians of our Indian frontier. As before, the stories have been carefully chosen,
for they who wrote them have long since won
their laurels in the field of literature, as some
of their number, indeed, had " won their spurs"

upon the field of battle. That their sketches will be welcomed for the old names' sakes is confidently believed, and that they will only serve to swell the list of friends and readers is as confidently predicted.

THE PUBLISHERS.

CONTENTS.

	PAGE
CAPTAIN DREAMS	9
By Captain Charles King.	
THE EBB-TIDE	49
By Lieutenant A. H. Sydenham.	
WHITE LILIES	75
By Alice King Hamilton.	
A STRANGE WOUND	113
By Lieutenant W. H. Hamilton.	
THE STORY OF ALCATRAZ	135
By Lieutenant A. H. Sydenham.	
THE OTHER FELLOW	153
By R. Monckton-Dene.	
BUTTONS	171
By Captain J. G. Leefe.	

CAPTAIN DREAMS.

CAPTAIN DREAMS,

AND

OTHER STORIES.

"If you're not more careful, Captain de Remer," said his better half—his much better half they called her in the gallant Thirty-third—"you'll get into a scrape some night from which even I can't extricate you."

"What's the matter now?" said the captain, dreamily puffing at his cigar, as he struggled hard to work his broad shoulders into the overcoat of his eldest hope—three sizes too small for him. "I suppose it's something about this coat."

"Not so much the coat," answered Mrs. de Remer, tugging energetically at the straining collar, then shifting her grasp to the right cuff and stripping it from his arm. "It's the man inside; and that's the colonel's cigar you've got between your teeth this minute, and he's laughing at you now."

"I thought it uncommonly bad," answered the captain, with a patient sigh; "but, if he will lay it close beside me, how the mischief can I help it? I haven't had a really happy moment since Wayne left the post. He was my one consolation—outside of this roof."

"And no one had a moment's peace while he was under it for fear of his next absurdity," replies madame. "On the principle that misery loves company, you and he are well matched. Major Wayne is the only man in the army more inane than yourself. He's been arrested as a horse-thief, and heaven only knows what's in store for you. Now *do* think what you're about to-night, John, or I'll be summoned to bail you out before morning."

Meekly the captain allowed himself to be "happit up" in his own new top-coat, his hat pulled well down over his eyes, and then he stepped slowly forth into the gathering night. "I'll leave the door on the latch, papa," said the lady of the house, as he lingered on the piazza without. "Now for your catechism. *Sure* you've got your night-key?"

Down went the right hand into the depths of the trousers' pocket. "Ye-es—— At least, I think this is it."

"And your commutation ticket?"

Another dive—into the waistcoat pocket this time, fetching out a flat, gray card-case. "In here," said he, briefly.

"And the countersign, in case you're challenged?"

"No-o—— Well, that is I had; but it's no consequence. The colonel's coming back with me."

"Certainly! else you shouldn't have gone. And now, if the Loyal Legion call for a few remarks, you——"

"They won't, will they?" asked the captain, with pathetic trouble in his big brown eyes.

"They said they would. You gave me the Recorder's letter, and I wrote out a neat and appropriate extemporaneous speech for you."

"Hah! yes, so you did. Got it all ready here to memorize, right in my waistcoat pocket, too."

"Well, be sure you memorize the right piece, and not begin, 'Ladies and gentlemen,' as you did the night you were installed."

The captain blushed. "Wayne did worse

2

than that," said he. "But here comes the colonel. Good-night, dear."

"Come back here this instant, you wretch, and don't presume to go without kissing me good-night. There! I presume the next I'll hear of you will be in the hands of the police. *Do* keep your wits about you, John; you can't always have me. Take good care of him, colonel, and don't leave your cigars or anything you value where he can accumulate them."

"All right, Mrs. de Remer," sang out the colonel, cheerily, from his carriage. "Tumble in, 'D.' Now, driver, go lively!" Slam went the carriage-door, slam-bang the de Remer's door, and then all was silence at Fort Emory.

A long-suffering woman was Mrs. de Remer, despite the fact that she was blessed with a devoted husband, with happy, healthy children, a bright army home, a comfortable income, a circle of appreciative friends and as few cares as often fall to the lot of woman in or out of the army. Her husband was at once her greatest joy and her gravest tribulation. He was a lovely, lover-like husband, the other women said. "*He* thinks *his* wife the sweetest creature that ever lived," they sometimes added, sigh-

fully, for the benefit of their own less appreciative lords. And, nevertheless, in his moments
of abstraction, which were many, Captain de
Remer had been known to say and do or to
leave unsaid and undone things which were
enough to turn gray the tresses of a woman and
a wife through sheer chagrin and confusion.
De Remer never drank, never swore, never gambled, never growled, never cared to wander from
his own fireside, never saw anything to especially
admire in any other woman's complexion, conversation, or conservation. Never, until his
wife herself pointed out some peculiar grace, excellence, style, or virtue in other women or other
women's children, was de Remer ever known to
admit it, much less—oh, that such wisdom or
oblivion were more widely disseminated!—to
remark it. "No one," sobbed Mrs. Darling,
"no one ever heard of *his* telling *his* wife that
Mrs. Flight, or any other woman except her,
seemed to look younger every day of her life."
Indeed was de Remer a model husband, but for
one ludicrous failing. He was the most absent-
minded man in all the army, except Major
Wayne, who was a bachelor, and therefore not
beyond hope of redemption.

Wayne's story has been told elsewhere. So long as he remained, Emory de Remer's otherwise vivid light had been hidden as it were under a bushel. But the major had been transferred to Fort Frayne, whence new tales of new absurdities were frequently wafted, and now once more had de Remer become the central figure of garrison anecdote, and time and again went up the laughing query, " What will he do next?"

But not even by long-suffering Mrs. de Remer could have been predicted the predicament of the night to come.

They went to town, the colonel and his faithful company commander, whom Blake of the cavalry had long since christened Captain John a Dreams, to attend the monthly meeting of the Commandery of the Loyal Legion, of which both were enthusiastic members. They met there choice spirits whom they often encountered. They met, alas! two old cronies of the colonel, transients, *en route* to the far West after a joyous leave in the States, and when de Remer would have readily returned on the " 11.30 suburban" to the barriers of Fort Emory and the bosom of his family, lo! it was the colonel who stood like a spread-eagle military angel, with flaming speech instead of sword, and barred the backward way to the Eden where he would be.

"Dreams, old man, I promised your blessed wife I'd fetch you home safe, and I'm going to do it, by Criminy! You're not to be trusted out alone this time of night. You're just as apt to get to walking in your sleep and turning up on the Pacific express or the Black Maria as you are to getting home—without me. Now I'll wire out to the post that we're coming on the fast mail. They'll slow up at Belt Junction to let us off,—I know 'em,—and my man'll go round and tell Mrs. de Remer, and it'll be all right. Then we four'll go round to the club and we'll have supper,—supper such as I've been spoiling to have with these two blessed old roosters ever since the Sioux campaign of '76. It makes me ravenous to think of it."

It made the colonel bibulous, too,—a rare trait in the old warrior, and the more demonstrative because of long repression. At midnight the up-stairs corridors of the Amaranth rang with the chorus of "Benny Havens O," and songs of other lands. The party was reinforced by a squad of club fellows ever ready for a convivial moment, and the nearer the time came for catching the fast mail the more was it apparent that the colonel wouldn't catch anything so surely as the curtain lecture awaiting him—with his headache—on the morrow.

"I've got to go," murmured de Remer to others of the party. "I'm on court-martial duty in the morning. I'll slip quietly out after a moment or two and leave the colonel with you. He'll be all right after a nap in the morning, and can come out when he's ready."

And that was the last seen or heard of "Dreams" for many hours. Colonel Stout stepped off the noon accommodation looking little the worse for the jovial revelry of the previous night, but his heart sank within him when his coachman said, "Where's the captain, sir? Mrs. de Remer said you were to bring him back."

"You don't mean to say he hasn't got home?" asked the colonel, in dismay. "I might have known he'd come to grief if he went where I couldn't watch him," he added to himself, with rueful forecast of what Mrs. de Remer would say and remorseful retrospect of the night gone by.

"Noa, sir; an' they've telephoning to town an' head-quarters——"

"The devil they have!" swore the colonel. "That shows how utterly damned inconsiderate people can be, and now everybody, from the general down, will know I stayed in town all night. Hold on, Jim! I'll call up head-quarters here from the depot."

It was a sympathetic aide who answered the colonel's telephone summons and not a gruff department commander or consequential chief of staff.

"Heard anything of de Remer?"

"No, not a blessed word—and the wires from Emory have been hot all morning. The police say no one answering his description has been run in. They say at the club he left there about 2.50 A.M., came in again in ten minutes looking as if he'd forgotten something and went out on the run, and that's the last they know of him. Colonel Tintop came down from the dining-room with him, but returned, they said, to rejoin you."

"Well, have you called up Tintop? I—I think he's probably in his room yet," stammered the colonel, and coloring despite the fact that his young friend was twenty miles away.

"Well, we've called, but he hasn't showed down," was the suggestive answer. "Guess his head's as bad as his hand this morning. He was to have taken the noon train for Omaha."

The colonel groaned so that the aide could hear it. " Is the general in his office?" he asked.

" Nope. Gone out for a bite of lunch."

" Well, say, Billy, there's a good fellow, just let on that I'm so anxious about Dreams I'm coming in on the first train. I'm blest if I want to face his wife this day, let alone my own."

And the aide-de-camp laughingly assented. The carriage went back to the post empty and the colonel to the city—full. Full, that is, of mingled anxiety, remorse, and resolutions. His first visit was to the club, and there he found Tintop, by no means the jovial blade he had parted with when they saw each other to bed at 4 A.M. Tintop was trouble up to the metallic summit of his head.

"I came down with Dreams because I had something to tell him," said that veteran yarn spinner, a man who would rather go without his dinner that be balked in telling a story; " and he seemed very much interested, despite his having to catch a certain train. He said he'd have to take a cab, and they ordered one for him at the office."

"But he was back in ten minutes, I hear. What was that for?" asked the colonel.

"They don't know. He went into the coat-room in a great hurry, and then came bustling out, jumped into his cab and drove off a second time. They rang up the cabman, and he said he drove the captain to the depot just in time to catch his train, and that's the last of him."

And to all intents and purposes that was the last of him until late that evening. Then at last there came a telegram to his half-distracted wife, "Am all right. Had absurd adventure. Tell the story later." And, very properly, her tragic grief changed instantly to glowing indignation.

And this—told with many blushes, and with not a few feminine comments, and with such evident mortification that for a time and to only a chosen few was it confided—was the purport of the captain's story.

Colonel Tintop was telling his yarn as they came down the stairs, and Dreams was dreamily listening, keeping up appearances of doing so even while furtively watching the clock. Distressed with fear of losing the thread of the story and thereby seeming impolite, and of

losing the train and thereby being derelict, de
Remer's already overweighted spirit was suddenly perturbed by the consciousness that it was
too late for the street cars, too far to walk, and
he must have a cab. Even while keeping up
a smile of simulated interest in the colonel's
monologue he managed to murmur a call for
a messenger. Then, *mirabile dictu!* he bethought
him of the lone ten-dollar bill that Horatia, his
wife, permitted him to carry as a reserve in case
of accident,—long experience having taught her
that money in any amount was sure to slip
through his hands. That cab, at night prices,
would be a dollar at least, and he hadn't twenty-
five cents in small change. The clerk accommo-
datingly broke the ten into a single five, which
he replaced in the flat card-case he carried in
the waistcoat pocket of his evening dress, and
a little stack of silver—dollars, halves, and
quarters,—which he scooped into the palm of
his right hand, while the colonel, clinging to
his left elbow, led him away into the coat-room.
The club must have been making a night of it,
for there were at least fifty overcoats of all sorts
and sizes hanging on their hooks; but de Remer
felt sure he remembered just where he had hung

his, the third hook beyond the mirror; and there it was, its change pocket invitingly towards him.

"Whatever you do, don't unbutton that overcoat and expose your unprotected chest to the night air," had been another of Horatia's parting injunctions. She had always held that officers had no business ever to wear evening dress, because their chests were usually so covered by their uniforms it made it doubly hazardous for them to wear open shirt fronts. De Remer was pluming himself on his thoughtfulness of her injunction, and thinking how unjust people were in accusing him of being absent-minded, when, even in the midst of one of old Tintop's long-winded yarns, he could think of his wife's admonitions. "I'll slip this silver into the change pocket," quoth he, "and then I won't have to unbutton the coat when I pay the driver." This he did forthwith, and then the colonel turned him round and made him listen to the climax of the story, which was long a-coming, and by that time the overshoes were on, and the servant, holding the overcoat in readiness, announced cabby at the door, and laughing heartily, as he knew how, at the *dénouement*, de

Remer hastily shook hands, bade the colonel good-night, ran down the stairs, popped into the cab, said "Great Western depot," and rattled off.

Before they had gone half a dozen blocks, and he was congratulating himself on having so deftly escaped the toils and taken all precautions, Captain de Remer clapped his hand to the change pocket of his coat—and found it empty.

Aghast he searched it. Not a penny there, and he could have sworn that not ten minutes agone he had placed five dollars in silver, heavy silver, in that very pocket, but, just to make certain, he felt in the other outer pockets, and with no result. There was not a cent in any one of them. For once de Remer acted promptly. "I see it all," he cried. "I've slipped it into some other fellow's coat. They were all bunched when I came out, and there were several very like mine, dark blue or black beaver with velvet collar. Back to the club, driver!" he shouted. "I've forgotten something."

So back they went, lively, for time was short. De Remer bounded up the steps. "I've forgotten something," he stammered to the servant who answered the bell, then bolted on through to the coat-room, and there—hanging on the third peg, just where he had left it—was the overcoat—his own overcoat he felt sure, and doubtless that stupid boy must have given him some one else's, some one of his own size, and he had never noticed the error until that most fortunate discovery that it contained no money. In an instant he was out of one coat and into the other,—a servant coming in just in time to pull down the disordered tails of his claw hammer,—then out again he darted into his cab. "Now, driver, for all you're worth!" he cried, "and it's half a dollar extra." He carefully counted out the promised silver and held it ready in his hand. The cab went clattering through the cold, deserted streets, bounding over cross walks, slewing around corners, and spinning over the massive bridge with the tall tower and the illumined clock disk of the station just coming into view. Only three minutes, by the immortal Joshua! Only *one* as they whirled under the archway, and, slinging the ready Jehu his shining dollar and a half, de Remer rushed madly through the waiting-rooms and out among the strugglers besieging the gate-keeper. Luck again! Here was his card-case (in which was his commutation ticket) in that change pocket, too. Something else was there under the silver! Odd! He thought that card-case was in the waistcoat pocket where he couldn't lose it, but, confound his mooning ways! he must have changed it before going up to the colonel's spread. Late as he was, there were others behind him. "Have your tickets ready, gents," shouted the lantern-swinging official at the gate. "All aboard, fast mail!" "All aboard, Omaha night express!" sung out the conductors underneath the dark train-shed. "Hurry up ahead there!" growled the hindermost gentleman, climbing up the captain's suffering shins. Blindly he tendered his yellow pasteboard to the gateman. "All right, Bulwer—First train to the left, sir. Hurry up, sir! Not a second to spare! Have to run for it now!" Bong! went the ponderous gong. Whoop—who—*ee* an engine whistled far to the front. "That's your train, sir! Help this gentleman up, Jimmy," and breathless, excited, and clutching his card-case in one hand, puffing, blowing, but successful, the runner was hauled aboard the rear platform and passed on into a crowded car.

It was filled with men and women, total strangers to him but on terms of familiar friendship with one another. Jolly chat, laughter, repartee, bright eyes, flashing teeth, traces of "make up" all too hastily removed, and de Remer understood it all in no time. It was some large theatrical company after the last performance in the metropolis moving on to the "next stand." Meantime with rapidly accelerating speed the train was whistling past switch-lights, thundering over crossings, darting under bridges, and then at last stretching away like a racer over the long tangents outside the city. "Bully train, this!" said the captain to himself. "Any other time we'd be stopping at every blessed one of these suburban stations. We'll be out to the Fort in forty winks, and I'll have the colonel's trap to myself. Shall I tell Horatia how I stowed the money in another fellow's overcoat, or made myself believe I did, and nearly missed my train? Well, perhaps not to-night."

A peal of merry laughter attracted him. One of the young men in the middle of the car was giving a capital imitation of a noted actor in Dr. Jekyll and Mr. Hyde.

The captain joined in the applause and shouts for more. The brakeman banged the rear door and came in. "Lucky we grabbed you, sir. This train don't stop for nothing when once it's going."

"Lucky, indeed!" said the captain, as he pressed one of the silver disks into the brakeman's palm; "but you slow up at the Junction, I'm told."

"Belt Line? Certainly, sir. Be there in five minutes."

"Bless me!" said de Remer, "that *is* going. I thought it was twenty miles out." But here another gleeful shout and clapping of hands took the brakeman away, and Dreams made for the rear door. "Horatia says never under any circumstances attempt to leave a train when in motion, but when I do to take the rearmost platform," said he to himself. A cloud of smoke and steam commingled closed in on the bleary tail-lamps; vague outlines of signal-towers, station-houses, and dim green and red switch-lights flashed into sudden sight and became dissolving views in another second. "No wonder they call it the fast mail!" said de Remer. Sometimes in the sleepy hours 'twixt twelve o'clock and reveille, when going the rounds as officer of the day, he had heard the roar and seen the rushing lights of this meteor of the night and wished he could do his weary mile of sentry posts in railway time. Another peal of laughter from within. What fun those people were having! and how little they'd miss him if he were to drop astern! A long blast from the deep-throated whistle far at the front. The captain grasped the hand-rail and peered cautiously ahead. The air-brakes began to grip the wheels, the speed to slacken. Belt Line Junction already? Incredible! Yet, that's what the brakeman said. Wonder why the fast mail should stop here, anyhow. A peep around the corner of the car, and far up forward were the lights of the station. Slower and slower every minute went the train. Then, at last, just as though decided not to come to a full stop, yet just as they seemed stopping, too, toot, toot far ahead went the whistle, followed by sudden hiss of air and release of wheels and sudden spring forward. "By Jove, she's going on again! Now or never! Jump, or be carried fifty miles without a stop!"

The next minute the captain's heels struck the icy space between the double tracks, then flew from under him. He brought up sliding, spread on his back and seeing stars innumerable in a clouded sky. His hat flew into the darkness. The precious coat—unconscious cause of the whole calamity—parted at the back under some intolerable strain; and when five minutes later, with the train already out of sight and hearing, the station-master was turning away for the night, he was amazed at the sudden appearance of a disheveled tramp asking for the colonel's carriage.

"The colonel's what?"

"The colonel's carriage."

"Carriage be d—d! You want the Black Maria."

"I expect I look so," said the captain, meekly. "I had to jump, or be carried fifty miles beyond the Fort."

"What fort?"

"Fort Emory, of course! The only one I know of near here."

"Fort Emory, your grandmother! That's twenty miles 'cross country, over on tother road. What a jag you've got, man!"

"Good heavens!" said Dreams. "Wasn't that the fast mail, and isn't this Emory station?"

"See here, Johnny," said the station agent, patronizingly, "you're as far off your base as any skate I've struck for a year, and it has been a good year for skates, too. Don't you know that's Number Four,—the Omaha express?"

"I don't know anything but that's the train I was told to take when I showed my ticket for Fort Emory."

"*You* got a ticket?" said the man, suspiciously.

"Certainly! I showed it at the gate, and the railway men not only showed me that train, but helped me onto it."

"Yes, you look as though you needed boosting," began the official, but Dreams's distress was too genuine to admit of his noticing so trivial a point. "How on earth can I get over to the Fort?" he asked.

"No way better'n walking," was the concise reply; "and the sooner you start the better."

"But I've lost my hat three hundred yards down the track, and it's dark as·pitch. I'd like to borrow your lamp a few minutes. Do you mean there's no train back to town?"

"Not before 6.30 A.M., and that don't stop. You left that hat with your uncle in town, Johnny, and you'll find the pawn ticket without a lantern. 'Spose he wouldn't allow you anything on the coat. You wasn't thinking of enlisting at the Fort, was you? You're too old a sinner even for them fellers."

"I'm very glad you can find any fun out of this," said Dreams; "I can't. Then can I wire to the Fort and find a place to sleep?"

"Not here," said the agent. "The operator goes home right after the express is signaled, and he's abed and asleep by this time. As for sleeping, what's the matter with the nearest barn? There's no hotel nearer than Prairie Lea, five miles east. What are you tramping for this time a night, anyhow? What you been stealing?"

"Merciful Powers!" thought de Remer, "what would Horatia say to that? I told you I came out on this train by mistake, and I jumped off when they slowed up at the crossing."

"You said you were ticketed for the Fort and the train hands put you aboard the Omaha. Now, I know they've no such chumps in the pay of this road. That story is simply rotten, Johnny. Come now, I want to close up."

"Before you do so," said the captain, with much dignity, "be so good as to favor me with your name, that I may report your language to your superiors in the morning. As for my credentials, here's my commutation ticket, and you can satisfy yourself." So saying he extracted the fateful pasteboard from his case and held it forth. The conductor had not yet reached the rear cars of the train when it reached Belt Junction, consequently, up to that moment, his ticket had been examined only by the gateman.

Uncertainly the agent took it, glanced contemptuously at it as though to say, "I size your bluff," and then, all in an instant, a keen, eager light shot into his face. He seemed about to speak, but with sudden self-control checked himself, peered under his shaggy eyebrows at the captain, and queried:

"How did you get this?"

"Bought it at the office in town."

"And what'd you say your name was?"

"I am Captain de Remer, Thirty-third Infantry, Fort Emory."

The station-master glanced keenly at him once more, then quickly shoved the ticket into

c

his pocket, saying, "You can sit here by the fire as long as you like. It's the best I can do. I live a quarter of a mile away, and there isn't a spare corner in my shack. 'Tall events you can't go anywhere 'cept by walking until 7.45, so make the best of it."

With that he let himself out into the darkness and slammed the door behind him. Dreams thought he heard it locked, but that didn't concern him. "The best laid schemes o' mice and men gang aft a-gley," said he with a sigh. "Now, what can Horatia be thinking?"   ·

Presently he took a turn around the room. There was the little ticket-office, closed and locked, both window and door. So was the door to the women's room adjoining. So, finally, was the door by which the agent had gone. "Verily," said Dreams, "I'm a prisoner, and nothing less," for every window was battened down tight and protected without by bars of iron. For the life of him he could give no plausible explanation of this. He would not have been surprised had the official locked him out, but why should he lock him in? And then it occurred to him that the station agent had gone off with his ticket.

Ten minutes or so he pottered about the room, half expecting the official to return, and at length, wearied, dejected, disgusted, yet philosophical, he seated himself in the arm-chair the agent had lugged out for him, propped his feet on the stove-rail, and presently dropped off to sleep. The last thing he saw or remembered was the white face of the clock informing him with a broad grin that it was 4.30 A.M.

Just at that hour half a dozen revelers came down from the upper regions of the Amaranth, were helped into their coats in the cloak-room and, further, into their cabs at the door. Just at 5.30 o'clock one of these vehicles with two fares, after certain intermediate stops, came to a halt at the Colonial Flats, and one of the two fares, after rummaging his overcoat pocket, startled the other and cabby, too, by saying,—

"By God, I'm robbed!"

At six o'clock the sergeant on duty at the Central Police Station was wiring to various sub-stations, and two detectives had visited Garritty's open-all-night oyster parlors and Madigan's Exchange, at both which popular night resorts the Hon. Jerry Brenham, M. C. from the Buckhorn District of the Prairie State, had tarried and partaken of good cheer, and been made acquainted with many prominent citizens on his flatward way. Mr. Brenham's loss consisted of a flat card-case containing his railway passes, four or five checks payable to his order, some valuable memoranda, a lot of loose silver, and about one hundred dollars in greenbacks which, rolled in a wad, was in his overcoat pocket,—the little change pocket on the outside. When asked how he came to have valuables in so exposed a point, the gentleman blushed. "Well," said he, "ordinarily I wouldn't," and the desk sergeant smiled benignantly.

"The chances are a hundred to one 'gainst our getting the money back, sir," said he; "but Garritty or Madigan, either, can recover the card-case."

And yet at 8.30 that morning Garritty and Madigan were both swearing stoutly that no one at their places had "lifted" anything belonging to Mr. Brenham. They were sure of it, because they knew every gentleman present at the time. At 8.40 they were still protesting, when there came a wire from Belt Line Junction saying a "snoozer" was there only an hour before who had one of Mr. Brenham's tickets, and the ticket was still there to prove it. The telegraph agent had caught a message ticking over the wires to certain station agents on the Omaha Air Line, at Bulwer and beyond, warning them and conductors to look out for anybody with the Hon. J. Brenham's "commutations" or "annuals," and here at Belt Junction had they run it down, and the bird was flown.

"Where'd he go?" wired the police.

"Back to town at 8.20. She was late. He bought a trip ticket. Said he was going to report me for impudence. You can nab your man at the Union depot if you're lively." Lively they were. Two officers were there when the train got in, but no one was visible who answered the description given. "A feller like that jumped off at Omaha Junction; said he wanted to catch the first train up the fort road," explained the brakeman.

"Well, run him down, follow him up," said the Honorable Jerry, who hadn't slept a wink and was resorting to stimulant again.

Cheerless, hatless, hungry, and mad all through, Captain de Remer had upbraided the station-master when that functionary came

4

around again in the morning to sell tickets for
the 7.45. There were few passengers. A
heavy snow was falling, and the train was late.
Dreams would have telegraphed the Fort, but,
argued he, " I'll go in on the 7.45, jump off up
town at the Omaha Junction, and take the Fort
local that comes along about ten minutes after
my train gets there. I'll be at Emory as soon
as my telegram," and so he would have been,
but that it was 8.40 before the 7.49 came buz-
zing and roaring through the drifts.

In his offended dignity, he would have no
more to say to the station-master, but he bought
a hat from a neighborly native, who was glad to
get a dollar for a Derby of the vintage of four
years back, and then kept out on the platform
until borne away by the train. At Omaha Junction he learned that he was much too late for the
Fort local, and it would be noon before the next
train. Here there was no telegraph, but some
shops up Erie street were suggestive of hot
coffee and rolls and steak, and even such as
they were they tasted palatably to the tired
man. Then he was directed to a journeyman
tailor who had a little shop not far away, and
into that artist's hands he confided the ruptured

overcoat, beseeching him to repair the long rent as speedily as possible, but that expert said it was a three hours' job; and while he was at it the captain begged permission to lay him down on the sofa in a little back room, and there he was soon placidly sleeping, so placidly that the noon accommodation went by without him, and this climax to a series of misadventures broke him up completely. Now he must wait until 6 P.M.

But not until one o'clock was the coat ready. He therefore decided to take the first train into town, where he could wire to Horatia, get a comfortable dinner at the Amaranth, and, after a shave and a hair cut, would astonish her by the trimness of his appearance when he got home. Back to the station went he, and a townward train had just gone by. No more for two hours and a half. "Go west six blocks and you'll find a trolley line," said a policeman, and so at 2 P.M. Dreams was whisking back to the treacherous core of the great city and pondering ruefully over the adventures of the day. "I am going," said he, "to the railway office and make formal complaint of that station-master, and also of the trainmen who saw my ticket and put me on the wrong road." And such was his intention when he reached the Court-House terminal at 2.45, but by that time he was hungry in earnest. The sight of ruddy lobsters, ice-rooted clams, and other sea dainties in the alluring windows of the Boston Oyster Parlors tempted him to enter. He dined. He treated himself to a bottle of Chablis, dreamily remarking how remarkably that little stack of silver lasted, and then to a cab to the railway office, where at 4 P.M. he inquired of a clerk where he could see the general manager. The clerk looked askance at the battered, browned, four-year old hat on the caller's head, and said the manager was busy. But the manager was a Loyal Legion man, and had most jovially bidden the captain to drop in and see him anytime only the night before.

"Is it anything I can attend to for you," said the clerk, somewhat airily.

"Possibly," said the captain; "but Mr. Roswell asked me to call only as late as last night."

"Oh, then, I'll take in your card," said the clerk. "He's dictating some telegrams at this moment."

And that reminded Dreams that not a word had he despatched to Horatia. He was thinking mournfully of this and not of the card as he drew one out of the flat, gray card-case that seemed unaccountably fatter; but Horatia often tucked in fresh supplies of cards when his pocket stock was running low. The clerk took it, started, got as far as the door to the inner sanctum, glanced at the card, then stopped short and looked curiously back at the visitor, who was now plunged in a brown study and seriously contemplating a railway map without having the faintest idea what was on it.

Still he could hear, and what he heard was this: "You tell Mr. Brenham that I've been bothered enough for one day, and if he has anything further to say to put it in writing. I haven't time to see him."

But why should the clerk come out and say to him "Mr. Roswell's too busy, and says to put your business in writing."

"I'll do it," said Dreams, irate once more, and asked for pen and paper and sat him down to draw up a formal complaint against the railway officials already referred to. It occupied him half an hour, during which time there was much coming and going. Then he arose, handed it to the clerk, who looked at him in a

4*

puzzled way even Dreams could not but notice.
Then he meandered off to the Amaranth, and
met a placid-looking citizen at the foot of the
office stairs who motioned to another, and between these two Captain D. was civilly given to
understand that a gentleman wished to see him
at the police station, in short, the chief himself.
De Remer wanted to ask questions, but the
"gents" displayed silver stars on their waist-
coats and utter indifference to his wishes in that
behalf and a degree of calm determination that
silenced remonstrance. In ten minutes more a
much aggrieved and bewildered captain of infantry was ushered into the presence of the awe-
inspiring head of the force, and that shrewd
official looked at once as surprised at Dreams
did bewildered.

"Sure there's no mistake?" he asked the
imperturbable "sleuths."

"None! This is the party. We tracked him
easy. You won't deny having spent the night
at Belt Junction and giving the station-master
this ticket, I suppose," said one, holding forth
the old pasteboard.

"Of course not, and I'm glad to get it again,"
and Dreams stretched forth his hand even as the

other gent deftly felt in that change pocket and drew forth the card-case.

"Here's part of the property, now," said he, to the chief. "What did you do with the hundred dollars?"

"What hundred dollars?"

"The hundred dollars that was in that change pocket."

"I never had more than five dollars there in my life, and came near losing that."

Again a prying finger and thumb were at work. "What's this, then?" said the officer, raking out a dusky roll, unfolding which he displayed a pad of ten and twenty dollar greenbacks.

"I never saw it before or knew it was there. Let me explain this thing. I took supper at the Amaranth late last night, and shoved some change into another man's pocket." (Here the chief looked incredulous and the deputies grinned with enjoyment.) "I discovered it in time, and went back to find that I'd got the wrong overcoat. I whipped it off and put on this, my own, which was hanging on the next peg, but somebody even more absent-minded than I must have thrust this money in here. 'Tisn't mine," said Dreams.

"Well, tell us something we don't know, Johnny," said one of them, with an affable smile. "Of course 'tisn't yours, neither is the card-case. The gentleman the coat belongs to 'll be here in a moment, and then you can explain further. That the style of hat they wear at the Amaranth?"

"That'll do, Murray," said the chief, in a cautionary tone. "You've sent for Mr. Brenham, have you?"

"Coming directly, sir."

Presently the door flew open and in popped the representative of the Buckhorn District. He was still flushed—with excitement, probably.

"Is this your card-case and money?" said the chief.

"It certainly is," said Brenham, looking thankfully at those items, and then in a misty, uncertain way at Dreams. "You don't mean to say—this—gentleman——"

"Nobody else," was the brief response.

And then the two gentlemen fell to studying each other's overcoat, then that which each was wearing, and then the latest arrival remarked, "Didn't I see you in evening dress at the Amaranth last night with Colonel Tintop?"

" You did, and I'm in evening dress yet," said Captain de Remer, throwing open his overcoat.

" And I'll be damned if that isn't my overcoat you've got on," said the M. C., " and this then must be yours."

The chief burst out laughing. " Gentlemen, do you often dine at the Amaranth ? Now suppose you introduce yourselves to each other, since your card-cases seem to have got mixed with your coats,—and possibly other items."

" By God ! Think of my wearing this all day, and never knowing it wasn't my own !" said the Congressman elect, contemplating with satisfaction the fine texture and finish of the captain's coat. " I think, so far as coats are concerned, I've the best of the swap."

" Then will you make it permanent ?" said the captain; " for I regret to say I met with a mishap and ruined yours, and it was all due to my unpardonable stupidity."

" Let's go somewhere and have a small bottle," said the M. C.

" Let me first wire to my wife that—I've been found," said Dreams.

*   *   *   *   *   *

Three days later the following letter was received at Fort Emory.

"Q. R. & X. Railway.
GENERAL MANAGER'S OFFICE.
"February 10, 189-.

"CAPTAIN J. A. DE REMER,

THIRTY-THIRD U. S. INFANTRY, FORT EMORY.

"DEAR SIR,—Immediately upon receipt of your letter of the 7th inst., the station-master at Belt Line Junction, Omaha Division, and the gateman at the Great Western station, were summoned to answer to the very serious charges preferred against them, and, after full investigation, I am constrained to say that, while the station-master frankly admits having used language which would have been most reprehensible, ordinarily, there appears to have been some warrant for his suspicions, as both he and the gateman declare that the ticket you exhibited was a Bulwer accommodation made out for the Hon. Jeremiah Brenham, M. C. elect. That the gatemen should have put you on the Omaha train was, therefore, their duty, and that the station-master should have failed to show you the respect due an officer and a gentleman is a matter which he most deeply regrets, and is most anxious to atone for, and which I can find it easier to explain to you in person if you will honor me by lunching with me at the Amaranth next time you——"

But here Horatia interposed. "The next time you go to town to lunch it will be with me, John; and as for the Loyal Legion and the Amaranth, we'll visit them when they introduce Ladies' Nights, and not before."

THE EBB-TIDE.

5 49

THE EBB-TIDE.

Lord Grosvenor and Mr. Edward Paget were sitting in a little smoking-room that looked into a brilliantly lighted ballroom in the country mansion of Sir Hugh Moffatt, Bart. The occasion was that of the celebration of the return of Sir Hugh from America, bringing as his bride one of the fairest of the reigning daughters of San Francisco. The air was stirred with strains of exquisite music, the production of finished artists carefully selected by Sir Hugh, and laden with the fragrance of innumerable cut flowers from the most renowned conservatories of London. Banners, jacks, and pennants drooped from the walls and floated overhead, reflecting in soft harmony the tints of colored lights shed from brackets and chandeliers hung in carefully chosen places. The gay company was in its most pleasant mood. The happiness produced by long drives in the clear May evening was heightened by the inviting brilliancy of the lawns and approaches of the mansion, lit with many colored lanterns, and flashing with torches, and by the cordial warmth of the reception that greeted each newly-arriving guest.

Lord Grosvenor and Mr. Paget, being gentlemen whose long contact with society had dulled the keen edge that finds delight in such gatherings, had slipped away into this little card-room, and were beaming complaisant approbation through the door upon the whirling mass of rich silks, flashing jewels, dress suits, and gay uniforms. Lord Harry had pushed back the ice and straws that remained from a mint julep, and was in the act of lighting a Turkish cigarette.

"Will you have a cigarette, Paget; or do you prefer to commit suicide in a more rapid manner?" inquired he, extending an enameled silver case of the questionable fumables.

"Thanks; don't care to smoke, my boy. Fact is, I'm thinking."

"Actually got an idea in your head, eh? Congratulate you! Don't wrestle with it too hard, or you will bring up in an insane asylum. Let's punish another round of this mixture." Lord Harry industriously pushed the button.

"Yes; that is, I'm thinking Moffatt must have had some deuced good reason for taking up with that girl. He doesn't need money, and he has been proof against some rushing heart-breakers in his day. Deuced queer, old man,—some good reason for it."

The progress of the dance at this moment placed Sir Hugh and his bride opposite the open draperies of the smoking-room. A soft, red light fell upon them from a chandelier overhead, and behind them rose the broad green leaves of a huge fan palm. Sir Hugh bent fondly over her a moment, waiting for the figure to begin. Her body swayed towards him, and her downcast eyes were lifted slowly and confidently to his; the effect was one of melancholy beauty. Tall, round, and full of figure, with heavy dark-brown hair, rosy cheeks, dark eyes and long ashes,—quite an impressive type of San Francisco loveliness. The music started the dancers whirling and the happy host and hostess were lost in the throng again.

The pair in the smoking-room had quit their glasses and sat staring through the doorway. Lord Harry rose and stood for a moment with one hand parting the drapery over the door, trying to catch another glimpse of her American ladyship. Then he returned and fell into his chair.

"Phew! Deuced pretty girl. Don't blame the boy. Have to congratulate him, eh? Ha! ha! Good reason, yes; fairly good. He married that girl for her looks." Lord Harry lit another cigarette and tipped back his chair.

"More than looks, my boy; there is a romance in it. Moffatt never tripped up on looks alone. I heard Wilston saying something about it the other day. When he gets tired of dancing a bit, we'll drag him in here and pump it out of him. Wilston says he met her at a hop at the Bear Island Navy-Yard, up in the bay of San Francisco,—you know,— that place where they harbor a lot of old tubs that look like Bedford whalers; and where it takes them so long to armor a cruiser that the style changes five times before they get it into commission. Deuced romantic place for a romance. I say, you go out and chase Moffatt in; you know him a bit better than I do."

"Well, you get things ready to entertain him at his own expense, and I'll try and fetch him. I'll have to apologize to him for being seen in

here with you,—of course, you don't mind?"
His lordship rose and waggishly twisted the
end of his moustache.

"Go on; don't be an idiot!" Mr. Paget replied, pushing his lordship through the door
and drawing the curtains after him.

In a few minutes behold the three comfortably seated around the table, with more mint
juleps and cigarettes in the centre. Sir Hugh
pushed back his glass with a look of pain.

"Why don't you youngsters learn decent
habits?" he inquired. "A few more of those
mint juleps and I shall be under the unpleasant
necessity of attending your funerals. Paget,
be good enough to push the button. So you
want to know how I came to marry, eh?
Can't stop long,—she might be looking for me,
—but I don't mind telling you; it was rather
odd,—quite romantic, you may say. Jones,
mix three Jamaica rum cock-tails, and put a
little Scotch whisky in them. You know—the
kind the American minister mixes for the
King of Greece; and be quick about it." Sir
Hugh bit off the end of a cigar.

"You see it's all about the ebb-tide, a favorite
little superstition of mine. My father was a

naval officer, and I was born on board ship
when his craft lay out in the Mersey, just as
the high tide was ebbing. That doesn't seem
at all strange, but father never let me forget it;
used to tell me when I was a boy that it was an
unusual thing. Then when I was at college he
and some of his men were killed in a boat while
chasing pirates into the mouth of a river in
Africa, and the ebb-tide brought the boat back
out to sea, in sight of the ship, and they put
out and rescued the bodies. After that, when I
was a subaltern in the Indian service, I was
ordered from Calcutta to join a small detach-
ment up the Brahmapootra by sunset of a certain
day. A part of the distance we were obliged
to make in a pulling boat; but the high tide was
ebbing swiftly, and we were delayed more than
three hours. On our arrival we found that the
native garrison had mutined, killed every Sahib
in sight, and took to the tall timber. If there
had been a flood- instead of an ebb-tide, I should
have gone to heaven as a representative from
Assam, instead of being here to instruct you in
the mysteries of Jamaica rum punch. These
little incidents, gentlemen, and some others
that I shall not take time to tell you of, have

led me to believe that the ebb-tide has some sort of propitious influence over my destiny; therefore, when I tell you that it is to the ebb-tide that I am indebted for my bride, you will agree with me. My regards, gentlemen; tell me how you like this, and I will continue."

"Elegant!" said Grosvenor; "mint julep isn't anywhere!"

"Capital!" said Paget, smacking his lips. "Where did you learn to make it?"

"An American chap from Philadelphia taught me the compound. Be careful you do not take too many of them." Sir Hugh lit his cigar. "I must hurry, gentlemen; some one will be hunting me presently. You will pardon me if I go on with the story?"

"Yes, yes; go on!"

"Well, you remember that I went to America with Wilston in his yacht 'White Wings,' and that he left me in San Francisco and came back without me. One day, while we were lying in the bay off Alcatraz Island, we received an invitation to attend a hop to be given by the officers of the navy-yard at Bear Island. As all had engagements to go out that night except myself, I determined to go and represent the party. A Mr. McWhite, of St. Louis, who had been calling on us, offered to accompany me; and I was glad to have his society, for he was a genial chap, and I dreaded to make the trip alone. He assured me that the train for Gallego, which is a town on the mainland opposite Bear Island, did not leave until half-past four; at which time we would be joined by some other naval officers from the harbor, and we would have quite a party on our way to the hop.

"I sauntered quietly about the yacht until a little after four, then had the launch pull alongside, dropped my valise containing my full dress suit into it, and steamed over to the wharf from which the ferry started. Leaving word with the coxswain that I was not to be expected back until the next morning at ten, I entered the ferry-house, purchased my ticket for Gallego, and began to hunt for my promised companions. To my astonishment, not one was to be found. Evidently they had boarded the ferry-boat, so I went on, and, leaving my valise with a porter, searched the boat over and over, still without success. Just as the boat was casting loose I went aft, and beheld, in the act of crossing the plank, my friend McWhite, with a valise and top-coat and a countenance too long to appear in a single issue.

"'What's the matter?' I exclaimed, embracing him.

"'Matter!' he gasped, blankly. 'Matter! Why, we're two blithering, blooming slobs! That's what's the matter!'

"'How's that? What do you mean?'

"'Why, we're left; that's all.'

"'You're mistaken; we're here. It's the rest of the party that is left.'

"Mr. McWhite cast upon me a look of mortal anguish.

"'I tell you we are left! The train we should have taken starts at four. All the rest are on it; they think we have given up the trip: there is no way of sending them any word, and there is not another ferry to Gallego until to-morrow morning. If you can fancy yourself left any worse than that, you must have a very vivid imagination.'

"He bitterly seized me by the arm and led me forward, where we both leaned over the port railing. A school of porpoises was sporting and blowing among the swells a short distance from the boat. Following them my eyes caught sight of a spar buoy pointing its long green finger towards the Golden Gate. All of the ships in the harbor were turned with their sterns to the sea, like a lot of impecunious gentlemen at a church fair in the presence of a subscription collector. Then an idea rushed into my mind: it was the ebb-tide.

"As I gazed into the water, the idea took possession of me, and every visible object forced the impression more deeply upon my consciousness. The ripples on the land side of the rocks, the surf beating on the shore, bits of wood and spars floating out to sea,—all contributed to thrust this one idea upon my thoughts and fasten it in my mind. I turned to McWhite.

"'We must go on,' I said. 'There is no turning back. Ferry or no ferry, we shall reach the island to-night. We must reach the island to-night.'

"'Go on; I perish with you,' he responded, resolutely.

"The boat touched the landing and we hunted a vacant seat in the cars. Not one familiar face met our inquiring gaze. The conductor, while taking our tickets, said that our train stopped at the ferry landing at Gallego Junction, but no more boats crossed until next morning; neither did he know of a single small boat or other means of making the crossing to Gallego.

"'We will cross if we have to swim,' I said. McWhite averred that, if it were possible to avoid it, he preferred not to swim.

"Then the train pulled away and left us standing on what proved afterwards to be the depot platform, and a sense of what it is to be in a place absolutely devoid of light settled upon us. I have been in the Thames tunnel when the gas supply gave out; and I was once left in the heart of the great Pyramid with an extinguished lantern, but never before had I understood that overwhelming sense of vacancy and dread which accompanies the total absence of light. Not a sound except that of our own footsteps and the rumble of the train dying away in the distance broke the stillness.

"'Why didn't we go back?' groaned McWhite.

"'Come on,' I answered, seizing him by the arm; 'it is too late for regrets now.'

"We slowly felt our way in the direction towards which the train had disappeared, not knowing what bottomless pits or hidden dangers yawned to engulf us. After about fifty yards of such progress our feet fell on gravel, and on looking up, we beheld the stars; then, a little to our left, the glimmer of a light.

"McWhite was ready to burst into tears; I could hear his suppressed sighs. 'Have you said your prayers?' he feebly inquired. 'Have my remains forwarded to my mother.' Then we struck out boldly in the direction of the light. Other lights began to appear, and soon we were aware that a village nestled in a pocket under the cliffs. Presently we encountered a pedestrian crossing our path, who, in response to our anxious interrogation, informed us that he would be glad to assist us in any way; that he was a Wiltshireman, and therefore glad to be of service to a countryman. It was four miles to Bear Island, and a difficult passage; but he knew of a single small boat owned by one Pete Johnson, who might be persuaded to row us over, provided the remuneration was sufficiently advantageous. The light we saw was at the village tavern, where Pete had his lodgings. We entered the hostelrie, and after a glance at the occupants there, tipped backed in various attitudes against the wall, concluded that there were neither philanthropists nor foreign missiouaries among them. As a precautionary measure we told the proprietor to ask the gentlemen what they would have, and during the excitement which followed this invitation we were presented to Pete Johnson. Pete rose, stretched his arms, and replied:

" ' Ya-as; I ha' got a bo-at. I yust get done work to-day, an' I be purty tired. I tek you 'cross for six dollar. The tide he be runnin' out, and it be purty hard to row up stream.'

" ' Come !' said McWhite, taking him by the arm. ' Come; there is not a moment to lose.' As he passed me, he whispered, ' Hurry up; let's get him off before he changes his mind.' We hastened down to the shore, where the surf was beating ominously over the rocks.

" ' Pete,' said I, ' it's a long pull, and you had better take a bracer before you start out.' I handed him a small flask that I had in my pocket. ' Can you drink out of a bottle ?'

" ' My mother she teach me to drink out of a bottle, an' I no ha' forgot it,' he chuckled. He made good the assertion by emptying the bottle.

" We entered the craft, which Pete held against the shore with an oar. There were three seats,—Pete occupied the forward one,

McWhite that in the stern, and myself the second; the valises filled the bow. Of all fragile crafts this was a little more so than any I ever entered; flat-bottomed, short, without a rudder, every movement threatened to capsize it.

" ' Have you an " Examiner" in your pocket ?' inquired McWhite.

" ' Yes,' I replied.

" ' Well, hold on to it; nothing in that will ever go down!'

" As he shoved off, it seemed as if we had joined Charon in a final journey across the Styx. The waves heaved troublously. A few lights were visible at distances which appeared very great; among them we detected the colored lights of vessels. A green and red pair appearing from the land side passed so close to us that the swells threatened to capsize us. Then we knew that we were in the track of the river boats, and we mentally parted our hair in the middle in heroic efforts to trim ship, lest we should be buried beneath the swells of some dark river phantom. I asked Pete if he knew the lights.

" ' A tenk so,' he said. ' I ha' made more

den fifty trips lak dis. De boat she pull hard when de tide go out.'

"I seized McWhite by the trousers to assure myself that he had not fallen overboard; he had not uttered a word since starting, but, although he was quiet, I discovered that he was easily riled.

"'For God's sake, keep quiet!' he ejaculated. 'You'll have us both at the bottom in a minute; and I don't care to present myself at the heavenly portal when there is any danger of Saint Peter's thinking that I am from San Francisco!'

"At this instant a heavy swell twisted the boat half round and doused us with water. I heard McWhite groan fervently.

"'It's all right, old man; brace up. The ebbtide never brought ill luck to my family yet!'

"To trouble you further with the details of that diabolical four miles would be wearisome. To go out in the dark, into the middle of a bay with enough wind blowing to stir up the white caps,—nothing between you and the bottom but a cockle-shell of a boat with a bungling Swede to manage it, all for the sake of dancing a few figures with a lot of total strangers,—is what any sane person would call rabid, blooming idiocy."

"Then what the devil did you do it for?" broke in Grosvenor, who could not contain himself any longer.

"Don't be excited; that's just what I'm trying to tell you," continued Sir Hugh. "You know that, according to popular superstition, if you turn back after starting to do anything, bad luck will follow you? Well, that kept us from turning back, and the ebb-tide idea in my head kept us moving on. I felt that something was going to happen,—just as surely as when a man touches a match to a keg of powder. So we kept urging that Swede like a jockey does a favorite on the last heat, until we were fairly under the guns of a big man-of-war that was lying at anchor below the island. We passed it a bit faster than the usual rate, and so close to the ship's side that we could see nothing at all to the starboard. Just as we rushed past the bowsprit, a huge black object leaped upon us like a locomotive on a parcel of rats in a tunnel, and in an instant more we were floundering in the water.

"We had been struck pretty hard, but fortu-

nately we were not separated. The black object
had taken us close astern, just behind poor
McWhite, and had turned the boat completely
over, spilling us out bag and baggage, quicker
than the whisk of a squirrel's tail. When I got
the water out of my eyes, I could see by the
light of the ship's lanterns that the boat had
righted itself and was floating right side up
about ten feet away, splintered somewhat, but
not entirely wrecked. Pete was in the act of
pulling himself over the bow, and McWhite
was threshing and struggling, first for the ship
and then for the boat, whichever in his mad
evolutions appeared next in sight. I was vigor-
ously treading water and shaking the brine out
of my eyes, endeavoring to collect my scattered
ideas. Pete had recovered an oar and was industriously rescuing the baggage, for the safety
of which, thanks to closely-locked leather cases,
there was little to fear.

"By the time we had drifted back opposite
the port gangway, the watch, aroused by the
unusual disturbance, was standing ready with a
line, and it was my supreme joy to behold Pete
catch it at the first throw, and pull himself, boat
and all, towards the ladder. A second and third

line received vigorous bites from McWhite and myself, and we were hauled in, drenched and bewildered, and more dead than alive, by the crew of the vessel that had been the indirect cause of our discomfiture.

" We were in the act of explaining matters as volubly as our chattering teeth would permit, when a large steam-launch rushed alongside and stopped opposite the ladder. I heard a woman's soft voice excitedly inquire :

" ' Do tell us; were any of them much hurt? were they drowned ?' Evidently this was the launch that had run over us, and there had been no wrongful intent on the part of the speaker, at least.

" We were still standing on the plank and the steps of the ladder, shivering and chattering and the water running off in streams. A naval officer stepped up from the launch and the outline of a lady's figure appeared in the door of the cabin.

" ' Any of these people hurt? Who are they?' the officer sharply asked one of the sailors.

" ' No one hurt, sir——' Before he could continue, I stepped up and interrupted him :

"'Allow me to introduce myself, sir,' I said. 'I am Hugh Moffatt, of the British yacht "White Wings," and this is my friend, Mr. McWhite, of St. Louis. We were on our way to the hop to-night when your launch ran into us. My friend McWhite is——'

"'Dead, sir; dead!' put in McWhite; 'these are his defunct remains.' His chattering teeth, however, indicated that life was not entirely extinct.

"'Come right aboard, gentlemen; it is impossible for me to attempt to express my regret for this unfortunate accident. You may discharge your boatman here or take him with you, as you prefer.'

"'How much have we damaged you, Pete?' I inquired.

"'I tenk about twenty-five dollar fix dat boat up dis time. I go no more trips lak dis!'

"'Very good, my man; you may go now,' I answered. 'We are indebted to you in a manner that cannot be repaid by money.' I managed to find the necessary coin.

"We entered the cabin minus our hats, the water running over the floor of the cabin, and standing in pools under our feet. Wet and bedraggled, we were sorry objects to look upon. The naval officer turned to the other occupant of the cabin, and, motioning towards us with his hand, said:

"'Miss Stanton, these gentlemen were on their way to the hop to-night when our launch capsized them. Permit me to introduce Mr. Moffatt, of the British yacht " White Wings," and his friend, Mr. McWhite, of St. Louis.'

"'I am so sorry! I hope you are not hurt! It is a very unfortunate way of making acquaintances,' said Miss Stanton, beaming upon us a smile of sympathy that would have warmed the heart of an Esquimaux.

"'Oh, no; not inconvenienced in the least,' said McWhite, holding out his fingers for the water to drain off. 'Little incidents like this are very common with us,—we always enjoy them.'

"'Yes,' I added, ' we will enjoy the hop more than ever for this little bath.'

"'Then you will not give up the hop? I am so glad! You deserve all the pleasure it is possible for us to afford you after this dreadful accident. Mr. Pell, you must take these gentlemen right over to my cousin's, Dr. Pigett's, quarters, and say he is to take care of them for me. He will be only too glad to do anything in his power to make you comfortable. You must promise to come to the hop, now.' The earnest look of entreaty in her big brown eyes would have disarmed opposition in a Zulu brave.

"'Yes,' I answered, 'when we get fixed up a bit, we shall be only more pleased than ever to carry out our original intentions. I am glad Dr. Pigett is your cousin. I have the honor of knowing him very well.'

"By the time the launch touched the dock, Mr. Pell stood waiting for us to land, and two able seamen, with our valises in their hands, were in readiness to show us the way to the Doctor's quarters. We bowed to our rescuers and followed them, after renewing our assurances that we would appear at the hop-room. Even McWhite spoke a trifle less sarcastically, and bestowed a second glance upon the owner of the dark-brown eyes.

"Our reception by the Doctor, who was a graduate of the Government Naval Academy; the truly courteous manner in which he placed his quarters at our disposal, and exerted himself to provide all that would add to our comfort

and make amends for the mishaps of the day,
produced an indelible impression in my mind,
and spoke volumes in praise of the hospitality
of the officers of the American navy. The
water had not entered our valises to any serious extent, so that shortly after nine we made
our appearance—a vastly improved appearance
—in evening dress, and were on our way to
the hop-room. As we entered, our glances
sought the owner of the brown eyes. Yes, she
was expecting us; the brown eyes were turned
towards the door and soon brought their owner
forward to greet us. It was at this moment, I
think, that America scored another victory over
Great Britain in her own waters,—a legal capture for the brown eyes,—and they have ever
since held undisputed possession of the prize.
It is unbecoming my present position, gentlemen, to enumerate the many reasons that
existed for the capture of the Briton; but Paget
has known me long enough to be certain that
they were excellent; and for the rest, as you
have already met Lady Moffatt, you must judge
for yourselves."

"But what did the ebb-tide have to do with
it?" interrupted Grosvenor.

"Without the ebb-tide, my lad, it would never have happened. The delay of our boat by the tide brought us under the bows of the 'San Francisco' just in time to be upset by the launch in which Miss Stanton was crossing to Bear Island. As she found it getting late, she had decided not to attend the hop, and had announced this, much to Mr. Pell's disappointment, only a moment before we were struck. Then her curiosity to see how we looked with the salt water out of our eyes, as well as her anxiety to assure herself that we were repaid for our accident by being made to enjoy ourselves, caused her to reverse that decision. Mr. Pell, although he doubtless felt himself repaid for his labors, was required to introduce us to the entire assembly, and to look after us generally in a manner that was an imposition upon the good nature of any white man. That was my first ball as the guest of American naval officers, and it was one of the memorable events of my life. They are truly polite, accomplished, hospitable,—a superior class of men; and my acquaintance since has not altered the impressions of that evening. But you must excuse me now, gentlemen; her ladyship will be look-

ing for me. I have told you the ebb-tide was
responsible for many things: among them, the
yacht 'White Wings' returned to England,
leaving me in San Francisco,—for my health;
and to-night it has afforded me the pleasure of
meeting you here. To-morrow at lunch, if you
will be good enough to remain, Lady Moffatt
will be glad to entertain you with her version of
the events of that night, and you will notice
that, although her name has changed since she
first met me, the color of her eyes has not; and
I think you will agree with McWhite, who said
that evening when he bade me good-night:

"' It's an ill tide that ebbs nobody good.'"

WHITE LILIES.

WHITE LILIES

WHITE LILIES.

SHE was very young, not more than seventeen, and exquisitely pretty, in spite of the damaging fact that her dress was in the very highest height of fashion, and she was the only passenger who got on board the " Mary Powell" at West Point. She carried a large bunch of fragrant fading white lilies—my favorite flowers —in her hand, and perhaps it was this as much as her beauty which caused me so particularly to notice the girl at first, but when once I had looked at her I found it difficult to turn my eyes away.

Around her throat she wore a pair of cadet chevrons, brilliant with gold lace, which she had arranged to form a very gorgeous collar. Her ear-rings were bell-buttons; bell-buttons dangled and rattled upon the bangles on her slender little wrists, and a number of the same shining spheres were skillfully fashioned into a scarf-pin.

" Evidently," I said to myself, " this little

maiden has been a favorite at the Point."
Presently she spread her fan, ornamented with
military designs done in brilliant water-colors,
as well as covered with autographs, and opened
a novel, between the pages of which I could not
help seeing that she had secreted a photograph;
and I smiled at the innocent device, which was
one I myself had not despised in days gone by.

I was half ashamed of myself for watching
her, as she sat so calmly unconscious of my
stolen glances, but she was so very lovely, with
her Titian-yellow hair, big, long-lashed brown
eyes, and fair skin, pink tinted like a shell;
and there was a look about her face which
strongly reminded me of one who had been,
and still was, very dear to me. Yes, she certainly *was* like Clara Avery. Could it be that
she was the little Lilian—named after me—
whom I indistinctly remembered as a delicate,
large-eyed little creature of six, eleven long
years ago?

"Highly improbable," I told myself. "And
yet, why might it not be?" Clara's home was
in New York, and this pretty maiden must be
very nearly of Lilian's age. I grew quite excited
over my fancy, and finally decided to speak to

the subject of it. At least I had an excellent excuse for so doing, and, in any event, I should like to know the lovely creature's name.

My camp-chair was not far removed from hers, and drawing it still nearer, I said, half apologetically, "Pardon me, but is not your name Avery?"

She looked up with a shy, inquiring gaze, and answered simply, "Yes, madam; my name is Avery."

I could scarcely believe that my fanciful conjecture had proved to be the true one. "And is your mother Clara Avery? Can it be that you are little Lilian?"

"Yes; mamma's name is Clara, and I am 'little Lilian,'" she replied, with a charming smile and blush. "Are you a friend of mamma's?"

"Yes; she is almost the best friend I have left in America," I returned, eagerly. "How strange it seems to meet Clara's daughter in this unexpected fashion! Would you believe me if I should tell you that you are named after me? Surely you have heard your mother speak of Lilian Reid—Lilian Thornton now,—though, of course, you cannot remember me?"

She was all excitement in a moment. "Oh, she is always telling me of you, 'Cousin Lilian,' as she has taught me to call you, although you are not really my cousin, are you?"

"Only by a certain marriage which made us cousins when I was much younger than you; but I have always loved your mother as if she had been an elder sister. Dear Clara! How good she has been to me!" And I gave a sigh to the dear old memories. "You look a great deal like her, I think."

"So every one says. But I thought you were in Europe, Cousin Lilian. · I may call you that still, mayn't I?"

"Yes, indeed," I responded, warmly. "Well, I have only just returned, and expected, during my stay in New York, to walk in upon your mother and surprise her, if she had not moved away since I last heard from her,—longer ago than I like to think of. She is well, I hope?"

"Oh, yes; thanks! And you—I do hope you are going to make us a long visit?"

"I have yet to decide where I shall take up a permanent abode. Perhaps it may be in New York; and if so, you will not care for a lengthy visitation. You know I am quite alone now, and very lonely, for my mother and auntie both died within two years after my marriage; and since my husband's death, four years ago, I have led a nomadic existence abroad, without any home and few real friends. I dreaded to return to America and find all so changed, but now I am glad I made up my mind to do so. And it is so pleasant to have met my little namesake in this unexpected way!"

Then ensued many questions and answers, and much friendly talk, so that an hour went by and seemed like a few moments.

"And so you have been to West Point?" I remarked, finally, with rather a mischievous smile, when I had heard all that she could tell me of her home and mother.

"Yes; I have been there for more than a month, staying with Major Eliot's daughter Jennie. It has been simply a *heavenly* time!" with all the *empressement* of seventeen.

"Do you know, dear, I almost envy you!" I exclaimed, with half a sigh.

"You envy *me*, you, who are so beautiful, and rich, and—and *everything!* I think you must be joking!"

"Ah, no! Am I not twenty-eight years old,
  f

and you seventeen ? Besides, you have just been to West Point, and I cherish most affectionate recollections of that dear old Paradise. I was so happy there once! I remember wondering when I left it, eleven years ago, whether, with all the future might hold in store for me of joy or triumph, I should ever know such perfect happiness again. I never have. Nothing has been like that, and never will be, for then the world and I seemed young together, now we have both grown old."

Her face paled and saddened a little. "Won't you tell me about that time ?" she asked. "You don't know how interested I should be."

"Ah, my little story is not half as interesting, I fancy, as one *you* might tell if you chose. You would not care to listen to it."

"Oh, indeed I should care, for ever so many reasons !"

"You would like to draw comparisons, perhaps ?" I smilingly suggested. But, after all, why should I refuse to grant her request? Why should I hold my poor story as too sacred for even these sympathetic young ears to hear ? It had all happened so long ago, and it was in nowise different from a thousand other silly girlish romances, whose owners soon lived them down. I ought now to be able to laugh over it as freely as the rest of the world would do, and yet, while I breathed the dying fragrance of those lilies, and looked out wistfully upon the beautiful familiar river scenery, somehow I *could not* laugh.

"Go and find a glass of water, then, for your poor lilies," I said, "for I can't tell a story while my favorite flowers lie dying before my eyes."

When she had done my bidding, I found myself compelled to keep the tacit promise, repented as soon as made.

"I scarcely know where to begin," I hesitated, "but perhaps it had better be with the arrival of an invitation to visit my Uncle and Aunt Ferguson, who lived a mile or two below West Point. How wild with delight I was over that invitation, and how my heart sank proportionately when poor little mamma sadly told me she could not possibly afford the money for my journey or outfit! My bright visions vanished in a moment, like the airiest of bubbles; but, though I gave up my anticipated pleasure meekly enough, I could not resist writing a doleful epistle to your mother, who at that time was the *confidante* of all my little troubles. Then, just as soon as it could possibly arrive, came a note from her, containing a pass she had begged for me from her husband's uncle, who, you know, was a very noted railroad magnate in those days. Dear Clara! How good it was of her! And yet, in the time that came after, I sometimes wished that my letter to her had never been written.

" Well, the arrival of the pass caused a grand family consultation regarding ' ways and means.' Mamma sacrificed her cherished wedding-gown, creamy with age, to my modern vandalism that I might have a pretty ball-dress, and the veil was devoted to the purpose of trimming. Aunt Mary laid at my shrine a black grenadine she had intended making up for herself; so, with two or three pretty muslins, my new outfit was complete, and I experienced more pleasure in its possession than I ever have since in the most elaborate Worth-made costumes. It was the day of the graduation hop when I arrived at West Point, I remember, and Aunt Ellen Ferguson was going. She looked at me in surprise when she first saw me,—a tall, slim girl of seventeen,—exclaiming, 'Why, here we have a young lady where I expected to see a mere child! I'm afraid I shall have trouble with you: you look dangerous. I hope, at all events, you are not a flirt?'

" 'We never know what we may be until we are tempted, mamma says,' I replied, demurely; and I but faintly comprehended when Aunt Ellen shook her head, murmuring, 'Oh, those terrible cadets! I doubt I shall have my hands full.'

"I had no ornaments to wear at the hop, whither Aunt Ellen proposed to take me; so, with her permission, I robbed the garden of half its wealth of fragrant lilies, to pin them on my dress and in my hair and bosom, and tried to stifle my longing for a pearl necklace and ear-rings to match.

" It was the custom then, just as it is now, I suppose, for the 'floor managers' at the hops to address strange ladies and bring up cadets to introduce to them, and so, though I knew no one at first, I had not been in the hop-room half an hour before my card was well filled with names. It was all so new and wonderful to me,—the brilliantly-lighted mess hall, with its

draping of flags of all nations, the striking
uniforms of officers and cadets, and, above all,
the glorious music of the band, which alone
would have sufficed to make me fancy myself in
Paradise. I forgot my lack of pearls, the thin-
ness of my silk, the limpness of my ancient
tulle, and was fain to believe (in spite of former
impressions to the contrary) that I must indeed
be the charming and fascinating person those
gray-coated heroes pretended to think me. But
pride, you know, is said to precede a fall, and so
it was with me presently when the conviction
was disagreeably forced upon me that I was not
as irresistible as, just for that one evening, I
would gladly have fancied: there was a cadet
who *refused to be introduced to me!*

"I could not help noticing him, for he was
handsomer than any one else in the room,
although he had rather a gloomy or preoccupied
air, and watched the dancing without ever joining in it. Several times I had chanced to meet
his eyes, and finally had been moved to ask his
name of one of my partners, so that when presently I saw the two speaking together, I fancied
I could guess the subject of their conversation,
and was not displeased. By and by Mr. Abbott

—I believe that was my partner's name—came back to me alone, and I immediately put a question which, had I been a little older, I should have left unsaid: ' Were you asking that cadet, Mr. Hancock, to be introduced to me ?'

" ' Ye-es,' he stammered, looking rather un-comfortable.

" ' And he wouldn't come ?'

" ' He said he didn't know how to amuse young ladies. He doesn't often dance, you see, or have much to say to any woman who isn't old enough to be his grandmother,' Mr. Abbott proceeded to explain. ' He's a good fellow, and a fine student, but he cares more for his " Math" than anything else. We call him " Diogenes" among ourselves. I shouldn't have spoken to him now, but I thought you might like to meet him, for the sake of the contrast, you know, to the rest of us fellows.'

" Oddly enough, I was not in the least of-fended because my acquaintance was not desired by the big, handsome cadet who cared for his ' Math' above all other things. I was scarcely piqued even, but I was interested and a little curious regarding the new species of young man to whom ' Diogenes' could be an appropriate

nickname. A little later I was resting under
Aunt Ellen's wing, and mourning the loss of
my breast-knot of lilies, which was sadly ' con-
spicuous by its absence,' when 'Diogenes' appeared with the missing flowers.

" ' These are yours, are they not?' he questioned, holding them out to me.

" ' Thanks!' said I, stretching forth my hand,
when suddenly he half withdrew his which
held the lilies. ' May I keep one?' he asked,
abruptly.

" ' If you like,' I began, when Aunt Ellen,
who had been conversing with a friend, turned
and saw my companion. ' Oh, Mr. Hancock!'
she exclaimed; ' then you have met my niece?'

" ' I have not had the honor,' he said, rather
stiffly, and to my embarrassment she immediately
performed the ceremony of an introduction. I
was half vexed, half mischievously pleased, for
had not Mr. Hancock brought this undesired
acquaintance upon himself? He need not have
been so scrupulously honest in the matter of
my lilies if my presence was something to be
shunned.

" It was nearly twelve o'clock, and the ' german' would soon be commencing over at the

academic building, and many people were already deserting the mess hall.

"'You have no partner for the german?' he asked.

"'Oh, no; I only came to-night, and auntie tells me that partners are engaged for this german weeks before the time.'

"'Will you dance it with me, then? though I warn you I am not a good partner.'

"After what Mr. Abbott had told me this invitation surprised me so much that I scarcely remembered the necessity of answering, but rising confusedly I accepted his arm, and we went away to the academic building.

"Miles Hancock was not like any one I had ever seen, or ever have seen since, I think. He did not talk to me as most young men think it their duty to talk to girls. He told me a few quaint stories about the origin of some figures in the german, and then—suggested by those, it may be—something of the two years he had passed in Germany before coming to West Point.

"Sometimes, when it was not our turn to dance, we went out and walked in the moonlight, and then, instead of watching its effect upon my upturned face (as I felt morally sure

8*

Mr. Abbott would have done), he gravely discoursed about Copernicus and Tycho Brahe, until he roused me to an unfeigned interest in subjects I thought I had discarded with my school-books a year ago. How childish and silly I felt in comparison with him! and how I resolved to get out my books when I went home, and learn to talk on topics he was interested in!

"'Your lily is faded,' I said when the german had come to an end; 'you had better throw it away.'

"'Oh, no,' he returned; 'I mean to press it and keep it. I should not have asked for it else.'

"'To remind you of this evening, or to make you smile when you think of *me*—and my ignorance?'

"'Of neither,' said he, coolly, quenching my incipient vanity. 'I asked for it because it reminded me of my home. I haven't seen any flowers of that sort for years; they were my mother's favorites.'

"'I hope you will not press the poor thing between the leaves of your "Mathematics," unless you wish to *dry* it utterly,' I said, laughing, to hide the fact that his last words had touched me.

"'No; I meant to put it in a nice little white-covered Bible my mother gave me. I thought it would be more appropriate to the lily—and to you.'

"'Shall I bring you some more lilies soon from my uncle's garden?' I asked, pleased with the little compliment, though I had the sense to comprehend that he had not intended it as such.

"'Thank you! but do not take that trouble. It is not very likely we shall meet again,—soon, at all events,—for I seldom attend these hops or show myself in society. I am not much of a ladies' man, as you may have divined.'

"'But I *hate* "ladies' men,"' I protested; 'and as for me, I am only a little girl, not a young lady at all. I wanted you to talk more to me about the moon some time.'

"He smiled, an odd, pleasant smile. 'There are plenty of fellows who will be but too glad to "talk to you about the moon," in a far different fashion from mine, and, you will think, a much better one,' he said.

"And then it was time to bid each other good-night.

"In spite of these rather coldly ungracious words, however, I did meet him again, both

soon and often; at least, we *saw* each other, but
he seldom or never sought me. I often found
him apparently watching me at guard-mount, at
parade, and at the few hops he attended, at all
of which places I received more attention than
was good for me from everybody save *one.* I
was piqued, and perhaps a little mortified, but I
was far too happy in my gay, novel life to care
just then more than that ' little.'

"At last, however, one night at parade, when
the cadets had been in camp for a week or two,
he deigned to approach me (for so, half scorn-
fully, half triumphantly, I put it to myself), and
said, abruptly, 'Are you fond of music, Miss
Reid?'

"When I had returned, 'More than of any
thing else, as I hear *you* are of mathematics,' he
invited me to remain and go to band practice
with him that evening. There was a particularly fine programme, he said, as if he searched
for an excuse for his invitation.

"'After all, then,' I exclaimed, mischievously,
'you have not entirely forgotten that I possess
an existence, and *might* have a fondness for fine
music. I quite thought you had forgotten all
about me.'

"'I *have* been trying to do so,' he answered, very quietly, 'but have decided that it is no use.'

"I was electrified, and made no reply, so he continued, 'Five minutes ago even I meant *not* to ask you, but—but now—— Will you go with me?' And for the first time in his life, I fancy, Miles Hancock was visibly confused.

"Well, I went with him,—perhaps to punish him, as I said, for trying to forget me,—and somehow we seemed to grow so thoroughly acquainted that night that afterwards everything could not help but be different between us. He began to seek me continually, for I spent the greater part of every day at the Point, with Aunt Ellen for chaperon, generally at first half reluctantly, as if he fought against his inclination, but finally gladly, eagerly, as if surrendering himself to an influence sweet as it was powerful; and if I began to care for him then, I had reason to think he cared as well for me.

*   *   *   *   *   *

"You have heard of the money my godfather bequeathed me when I was a young girl, have you not? Well, it was during my stay at West Point that I received tidings of his death, and of the unexpected contents of his will. I was too wildly excited over my Cinderella-like fortune to be discreetly reticent, and so the news of my heiress-ship spread like wildfire among the gossips of West Point.

"I was quite anxious to hear what Mr. Hancock would say and think, but suddenly, without explanation, he began to avoid me again, never rudely or abruptly, but nevertheless his avoidance was unmistakably certain. I was hurt and perplexed, and when it had gone on for what seemed to me a very long time, I found myself heavy of heart and sad, for reasons I dared not try to read. At last we came upon each other in the library building, where I had been bidden to wait for Aunt Ellen.

"'Do you hate me lately?' I asked, with a sort of shy audacity, as for an instant he held my hand.

"'*Hate* you! most certainly not,' very gravely. 'Is it true, as I have heard, that you have come into a fortune, are a great heiress?'

"'Yes, indeed; isn't it like a fairy tale? But what has that to do with my question?'

"'Everything to me; it has essentially changed everything for me.'

"'Why?'

"'Because I had meant to ask you to marry me.'

"'And now you will not, just because of my *money ?*'

"'No; I will not, I cannot,' he began, but I interrupted him, impetuously, scarcely knowing what I said.

"'Then *I must ask you to marry me!* Please do,—that is, if you really still care enough for me to wish to! I shall be *so* unhappy if you don't!' And with tears and agonized blushes I laid my hands on his.

*   *   *   *   *   *

"When Aunt Ellen came in, ten minutes later, I had given him my promise, or he had given me his, I scarcely know what to say under such confused circumstances, but, at all events, we were engaged. Miles would gladly have told her immediately, but I would not have it so. She would laugh, and call us over young and foolish, I knew; say, perhaps, we had no right to engage ourselves so, and that I could not bear. It must remain a secret, all our own, till I went home again, and then mamma must be the first to know.

"After that there were two weeks of happiness for us both, happiness far too unalloyed to last. One evening there was to be a hop at the hotel. Miles and I were speaking of it two days before, and he wished me to promise not to go, as he didn't think he should be able to be there. He expected to be detailed for the observatory that night, and, of course, I was enough in love to give the required promise willingly.

" 'But then I sha'n't see you for two whole days,' I objected, 'as I can't come up to the Point to-morrow, and the day after, if I'm not to attend the hop, I suppose Aunt Ellen will say it isn't worth while for me to come at all.'

" ' Well,' he said, ' I'm sure of you now, and I hope we shall have lots of other days to spend together before you go away.'

" But he was mistaken.

" Aunt Ellen had not played chaperon for me that day, and when I reached home I found her with unexpected company, a Mr. Thornton, from New York, who had come once or twice before to the house during my visit.

" 'I've just been promising Mr. Thornton that you will go with him to the hop day after to-morrow,' she informed me; 'for I have prevailed upon him to stay over with us on purpose.'

"'But—but I'm not going to the hop,' I stammered.

"'Not *going!* Pray, why is that?'

"'Because'—hastily framing an excuse which at least was not an untruth—'I've just told Mr. Hancock I wouldn't go; and as he makes out my hop cards, I should get very little chance to dance if I changed my mind now that he doesn't expect me.'

"'Oh, no matter for that this one time,' persisted Aunt Ellen, impatiently. 'You will enjoy it well enough, I dare say, and perhaps Mr. Thornton may put down his name in the blank spaces on your card.'

"'With great pleasure,' came emphatically from Mr. Thornton.

"'Oh, but how it would look to Mr. Hancock if I should go now, when I've just positively announced that I would not be there. He will think I did it on purpose to avoid him,' I protested, more warmly than prudently.

"'Mr. Hancock will probably not give it a thought. At all events, I particularly desire you to go, my dear,' Aunt Ellen said, decidedly.

And she always said 'my dear' when she was
growing a little angry, even to her husband.
As for me, I was quite a child in her eyes, and
no doubt a troublesome one.

"'Well,' I said, 'then I must write him a
note of explanation.'

"'Write to Miles Hancock! a young man you
have been *slightly acquainted with for two months!*
I cannot possibly permit it!' ejaculated Aunt
Ellen, in horrified accents, which I thought quite
too exaggerated, while Mr. Thornton became
absorbed in gazing out of the window.

"'I can't allow my niece's handwriting to be
in the possession of any cadet, no matter how
nice he may seem to be. How can you tell
what use he might make of it?'

"This was too ridiculous, I thought; but
words were vain, and I relapsed into a discreet
though angry silence, being none the less resolved, since I must go to the hop, to write
Miles an explanation. I fancied I knew him
well enough to be quite certain of his being
vexed and misunderstanding me if I did not,
especially as I was to go with Mr. Thornton,
who was known at West Point as being wealthy
and a grand *parti.*

"I was quiet all the evening, intent on laying my little plot; and very, very early next morning, stealing down to the deserted library, I hastily wrote two letters, one to Miles and one to your mother, Clara Avery. The latter was to serve as a ' decoy,' if necessary.

"I had finished the first and secreted it in my pocket, and had commenced the other, when the door opened, and Aunt Ellen peeped in suspiciously, her hair still in crimping-pins.

"'I thought I heard a noise, and fancied it was you,' she said. 'Surely, Lilian, you are not writing to *that cadet* after all I said to you?'

"It seemed to me quite an insult to Miles that he should be mentioned as ' that cadet,' and with the courage of anger, though my heart throbbed violently, I answered, stoutly, 'No; I'm not writing to *any* cadet, but to Clara Avery.'

"She gave me a long, doubtful look, and, slowly turning, left the room.

"Never had I felt so utterly at a loss for something to say in a letter to Clara. I had no reason for writing, and after having set down ' Dear Clara' and the date, I looked at the page for a long time in despair, with my inky pen suspended, ready to dash down any fugitive idea which might occur to me, before I could think of a thing to say.

"Finally, I had not succeeded in completing my note, which seemed likely to be a lame affair, when Uncle Henry entered. As a rule, he was a particularly late riser, and so I knew Aunt Ellen must have used cogent arguments to induce this early appearance of his.

"'Lilian,' he said, very gravely (Uncle Henry was always grave, though kind, and he always spoke directly to the point), 'will you tell me to whom is that letter?'

"'To Mrs. Avery,' I replied, ostentatiously directing my envelope, and feeling sadly conscious of that other in my pocket. But perhaps my voice trembled.

"'And is that the only one you have written?'

"How sick I felt as I finished writing that address! For an instant I did not answer, then I said, faintly, 'Yes.' It was my first falsehood.

"'You are sure? Forgive me, Lilian.'

"'Yes; *sure!*' I cried, miserably. 'What a—what a *fuss* you and Aunt Ellen are making about nothing! My head aches, Uncle Henry, and I'll take my letter to the post-office now, for the sake of the walk before breakfast.'

"He made no comment, and I started off, not feeling as if Miles's letter were absolutely safe until I had left it at the Highland Falls post-office, with the assurance that it would soon be sent off to the Point.

"Uncle Henry once in a while indulged in a 'constitutional,' as he called it, before the nine o'clock breakfast, and I had been relieved when he had not offered to join me in my walk. Now, as I was rapidly returning to the house, I met him, and he stopped me, with a hand upon my arm.

"'Perhaps you will think me over particular in the matter of this letter,' he said, kindly, 'but your aunt has been impressing it upon me that it is absolutely my duty to be so, and you know how strict she is in her ideas regarding propriety. I don't know but I must agree with her; and now, Lilian, it is not too late yet. If you've put a letter to this cadet in the office, tell me, and I can go and get it out for you.'

"I was aghast as well as angry. I had fancied my letter safe at last, and now here it was in greater peril than ever, perhaps. Again

I protested I had written no such letter, but when he announced his intention of proceeding to the post-office to inquire for his own mail, I offered to accompany him with a fainting heart. To my joy he stepped into a grocer's shop on the way, and, framing some hasty excuse, I rushed out and sped away to the post-office, where I sought the post-master at his little window.

"'I—did you see me post two letters here a few minutes ago?' I questioned, desperately, all the time feeling heartily angry with myself and everybody else, even *Miles*, because of the position in which circumstances and cowardice had placed me.

"'Yes; I saw you, miss,' was the answer.

"'Then,' stammering and blushing furiously, 'if—if a gentleman—Mr. Ferguson, I mean,—comes here and inquires or asks to see them, you—you will not——'

"'Oh, no,' he interrupted, with an intolerably airy patronage and a smile so broad that his cigar trembled between his teeth. 'I know what you mean, of course, miss. Parents and guardians often come to us for such things, but we know how to keep our mouths shut; our memories are awful short sometimes.'

"I thanked him with a doubtful grace and returned to my uncle feeling utterly, shamefully humiliated, yet not wholly repentant. They had had no right to take me so to task, I reflected, and, after all, I had done no great wrong.

"But when, after breakfast, the family assembled for prayers and I knelt with the others, I was positively frightened, so like a Pariah did I feel. How good they all seemed! and *they* never told lies. I had told one, and I had no longer a place among people who dared to say prayers. Poor little wretch that I was! I feel almost sorry for my naughty yet remorseful self as I recall my misery. I was very unhappy till the night of the hop, and then I grew frightened again. If Miles should be there after all, and chance to mention my note to Aunt Ellen, what would become of me?

"We went early to the Point,—Aunt Ellen, Mr. Thornton, and I,—for we had been invited to dine with the family of one of the officers, and I distinguished myself at table by starting when I was spoken to, dropping my fork under the table, and even upsetting a glass of water into my neighbor's plate, to such a state of nervousness had I arrived. Aunt Ellen was thoroughly ashamed of me, I know.

"Well, Miles was at the hop, the night being too cloudy for work at the observatory, and in a breath with my first salutation I whispered, 'For pity's sake, don't mention my note!' and so succeeded finely in puzzling him and rousing his curiosity.

"It was quite a relief, by and by, to confess the sin I had committed for his sake, and to pour into his sympathetic ears the history of my sufferings and remorse.

"'Did he think me *frightfully* wicked? Could he ever love me again after I had told such a lie?'

"He managed to pour balm upon my wounds, yet said that were he in my place he would tell Aunt Ellen all about it now. I would feel happier, and it would be better in every way. A lie was a bad thing, he said, and one ought to do all in one's power to atone for having told one, even if it had seemed excusable at the time.

"'You're not a coward, are you, Lilian?' he asked, when I demurred; and after that I would rather have died than not have told Aunt Ellen. I did confess the very next day, in the presence of Uncle Henry (as an additional penance), and, alas! she was very angry. She spoke of the great responsibility I had been to her, with my 'appearance and unfortunate passion for flirtation,' as she emphatically expressed her opinion, and my mother so far away.

" ' I was frightened as soon as I saw you,' she told me, ' for I had never realized that I was to have a young lady on my hands, and I doubted I should have trouble with you. Now it has come. You have chosen to deceive us, and what you have done once there is no reason to believe you may not do again. I don't dare to keep you here any longer, I tell you honestly, though I don't wish to seem unkind, and I must write to your mother to send for you directly. It is for her sake, as well as for yours and mine, that I do it.'

" I was in despair at this decision, though too proud and angry to remonstrate or attempt to defend myself, still less mention the fact of my engagement as excuse for what I had done.

" So I was sent home in disgrace, without even the privilege of one sight or word from Miles Hancock, for I was not allowed to show myself again at the Point, so dangerous a person did my aunt now consider me.

"When mamma had been told of the important fact of my engagement, and had received a long and (in my opinion) *beautiful* epistle from 'my cadet,' her heart being much softer than Aunt Ellen's, we were allowed to write to each other sometimes; and the next June after his graduation he came and spent a week in the lovely new home my 'fortune' had procured for us.

"And there, Lilian, I will close my little story. That is the way, isn't it, they do in the magazines,—leave the hero and heroine in a halo of happiness and indefinitness? Now you have the only romance in the experience of this sadly unromantic person, and you must remember it is your own fault if you have been bored. As for me, I have talked myself into the dreariest mood imaginable. It always makes me a little sad, foolishly so, to recall those old days at West Point." And I sighed involuntarily as I bent over Lilian's flowers.

"But surely that is not the end, Cousin Lilian?" cried the girl. "Won't you tell me what came be—— but, oh, no, I ought not to ask that."

"Oh, yes; you are at liberty to ask;" I tried

to speak with smiling indifference. "There came a quarrel, and then a separation. When by a chance we discovered that it had all arisen through a misunderstanding, a mistake, trifling enough if it could have been remedied before it was too late, I had already engaged myself to another man. Of course a promise of marriage, once having been made, could not be canceled because I had found out that I needn't have broken my engagement with some one else beforehand; and so there was the end of it all. A mere bagatelle, of course, a little dream of one's first season, you understand, Lilian?

"Ten years ago, and I have never seen or scarcely heard of Miles Hancock since! I dare say he is married, and the happy father of half a dozen noisy children," and I laughed. "Now, dear, have you not some little confidence to give me as reward for my dull narration?"

"Just a very little confidence, then, if you care to hear, though of course it seems a great deal to *me*," Lilian made blushing answer. "I am engaged to a cadet! And he is *such* a dear boy, Cousin Lilian,—you've no idea! Mamma doesn't know yet. I am going to tell her to-night, and you must help me if she scolds, won't you?"

"Oh, certainly; you will have an advocate in me," I answered, laughing. "May I hear his name, or is that to be a secret from me as yet?"

"First" (and I thought she seemed oddly agitated and nervous, as indeed she had seemed during all the progress of my story) "I will show you his picture. I carry it—don't laugh! —inside this novel. Perhaps—perhaps you may have seen him, or some one like him, before, you know. Anyway, I hope you'll think him nice-looking." And timidly yet eagerly she laid the photograph in my hand.

I took it, and I did not speak; I *could* not. The pictured face swam before my eyes, and yet another, so strangely resembling it, seemed to rise between me and the paper, like the ghost of other days. If ever I had told myself it was forgotten, I knew now that I had been deceived.

"Lilian," I asked, after a pause which seemed long to me, and my voice sounded strangely in my own ears, "how did *you* get this picture?"

"It is the picture of *my cadet!*" she cried, "and his name is Ned Hancock."

When I did not speak, she began again, "Haven't you *any* questions to ask me, Cousin Lilian? Oh, I *wish* you would ask me just *one!*" growing more and more excited and eager. "Ned's elder brother, Captain Hancock, is named Miles, and they are so much alike, even yet, though the captain is a very great deal older. They say at the Point that Ned is almost precisely like his brother in appearance when *he* used to be a cadet. And Captain Hancock isn't married, and he *hasn't* half a dozen children! He's home now on sick leave from his post in Montana, where he received a dreadful wound in a fight with the horrid Indians. Ned told me all about it, and he was so brave and grand,—you have no idea! He is stopping at Cozzens's Hotel this week, for the sake of being with his brother Ned, and we are great friends. He is coming to speak to mamma about Ned, day after to-morrow, and then— then, Cousin Lilian, you and he will meet,—you can't help yourselves! It is too romantic and lovely for anything! Now all will be made up between you again, and be just as it used to be, and I'll be so happy!"

"Hush!" I said, checking the girl's impetu-

ously incoherent outburst in a tone that was
purposely cold, though I was conscious that my
cheeks were burning and my eyes shining with
a long-unkindled light. "That little episode is
a thing entirely of the past. I was very foolish
to repeat it, I fear, and certainly should not
have done so could I have dreamed you had any
connection with the name of Hancock. Captain
Hancock and I—since that is his title now, you
say—are as little to each other as if we had
never met. You must——"

"At least," Lilian broke in again, reproach-
fully, "poor Captain Hancock has been and is
faithful to you, whatever you may feel towards
him, for he has never married; and I have
heard some of the professors' wives talking
gossip about some 'early disappointment,' from
which he has never recovered. I know *now*
that that means *you*. He is splendid, and I do
hope you won't be so horribly cruel as to refuse
to meet him when he comes to see mamma! If
you only once *meet* him, Cousin Lilian, I feel
sure of all the rest."

"Lily, silly child!" I exclaimed, with a smile
and a sigh, "don't you know that flowers once
withered never more revive?"

For an instant she was silent. Then, with a seeming irrelevance, she cried, her voice trembling ever so little, " Oh, see, Cousin Lilian, my lilies that had faded, how bright and beautiful they are again !"

Have flowers prophetic souls ?

A STRANGE WOUND:

A STORY OF THE REBELLION.

A STRANGE WOUND:

A STORY OF THE REBELLION.

SOME years ago, when stationed in a little town in one of our Western States on college duty, it was my pleasure and delight to spend my leisure hours after drill in the office of a local practitioner, a Dr. Brown by name. He had been a surgeon and medical director of a Western military district during the war, and had, moreover, a wide experience in various capacities. Possessed of great conversational powers, a close observer of men and events, a deep thinker and a great reader, his statements of what he had witnessed not only were of great interest, but remarkable for accuracy and truth as well as detail. One day while in his office the conversation took a professional turn, and he spoke of strange accidents and wounds, and ended by giving me the following tale, which I here relate in as nearly his words as I can now recollect.

" Well, lieutenant, one of the most remark-

able wounds I ever came across was connected
with a young fellow who belonged to this town.
It was in 1862, and I was then attached as
surgeon to a regiment of Sanborn's brigade,
Hamilton's division, in Rosecrans's Army of the
Mississippi. All through that summer and
early fall we were pretty scarce of medical
officers in that army, and I had plenty of work
to do, I can assure you. In September I was
appointed an assistant medical director, and had
my quarters on the staff of General Hamilton.
During the summer we had not moved around
much, but when the fall came, our work commenced in earnest. We were at that time in
Northern Mississippi, and Grant, who commanded the Western armies then, had an idea
of making a forward movement just the moment he felt himself strong enough. By the
capture of Forts Donelson and Henry, Island
No. 10, and the battle of Shiloh, he had cleared
not only Kentucky but all of Northern Mississippi of the Confederates, and also all of Western Tennessee. But in Eastern Tennessee Bragg
had a strong force, and threatened to start
northward and carry the war to the Ohio border. Now, Grant thought that if Buell could

keep Bragg in check he—Grant—could then
march southward and compel Bragg to either
retreat precipitately or find himself between
two large armies, and thus be compelled to fight
against great odds. I have always thought that
was a mistake of Grant's, for at that time if
he had consolidated his forces he could have
marched on Vicksburg and Port Royal, which
were then without intrenchments or much de-
fense, and have captured them with ease, thus
opening the Mississippi and saving the many
lives and battles of the year following. At
least, that is my opinion, but I am only a doctor, and I suppose my opinion wouldn't count
with military men. The forces Grant had in
September in his front and opposed to him were
Earl Van Dorn's army at and around Vicksburg,
and Sterling Price in his direct front in Central
Mississippi. The two together numbered about
thirty-four thousand men, while Grant had
nearly forty thousand, but spread out from
Memphis in Tennessee to Bolivar in Mississippi.
Now, when Bragg found Buell too strong to
pass, he could not break away from him, as
Buell would have kept on his heels, and between Buell and Grant he would have been

crushed. So he sent for Van Dorn and Price to
join him, and in order to keep Grant away he
ordered them to make a diversion in his favor
by breaking through Grant's lines. Well, now,
lieutenant, I am telling you all this in order that
you may understand why the battle of Iuka
was fought, a battle which, to my thinking, was
one of the most important in the war, though
the numbers engaged on either side were
very small. You see Grant had his principal
depot at Holly Springs, and at Memphis was
Sherman with sixteen thousand men, while Ord
and Hurlburt held the rest of the line with only
about sixteen thousand men. For a while Rosecrans had about eighteen thousand, since the
forces at Bolivar were put in his command.
After Van Dorn had fortified Vicksburg somewhat he started to make a break to the north,
and his first step was to seize the depot at Holly
Springs and then appear to march straight for
Bragg. But he was a sly old fellow, and instead
of marching at once to join Bragg he and Price
agreed to form a junction at Iuka, close to
Grant's lines, then breaking through his lines,
to roll Grant back to the Tennessee and northward, and then join Bragg, by which means

they would have been able to whip Buell, and thus cause a loss to the Union forces of all of Tennessee and Kentucky,—an amount of territory which had taken our troops two years nearly to gain. In that case, also, Grant never would have been heard of as a great general. So you can see the importance of Iuka. If it could be held long enough for Grant to get up his forces there in strength, then Van Dorn and Price would necessarily be compelled to retreat, and Bragg would not have his expected reinforcements. Grant penetrated Van Dorn's plan, however, but only two days before the battle, and he also sent forces to seize and hold Iuka, so that it virtually became a race as to who should get there first. Van Dorn made it, and at once fortified himself strongly, thus hoping to beat the forces sent against him in detail. He got in September 18, 1862, and the battle took place the next day.

"Well, now that you know pretty well the situation of Iuka, I will tell you my story. In 1859 Jim and Tom Ainsworth, twin brothers, lived here. They were a mighty handsome couple, both straight, tall, and well formed, and having good, manly faces. Jim was dark,—

that is, he had dark eyes and hair,—while Tom had blue eyes and hair a shade lighter than Jim's. They were both of the same height and build, and both were well educated and full of good sense. Well, you know the widow living over on the corner of Third and Washington Streets. She was Mary Carter in those days, and as pretty a picture of health, happiness, and good looks as the sun looks upon. Of course all the young fellows in town were wild after her, but it was some time before she showed a preference for the Ainsworth boys. However, it was a puzzle to know which of the two she liked the best. If she went with Jim one day, the next she was with Tom, and, notwithstanding this shifting, there did not seem to be the slightest jealousy between the two brothers. Sometimes all three would come into church together, and after service was over she would smile as much upon one as the other while she walked home with both. I used to watch them pretty often, and, somehow or other, I fancied it was really Tom she liked the most, though I could not tell why, and she must herself have been unconscious of it.

"Things went on that way through the year,

and then came the talk about Breckinridge,
Lincoln, and Douglas. The brothers were both
Southern, and of course looked at matters from
a Southern point of view, and they went about
making speeches together and helping along
each other all they could. They were both
smart lawyers, and having come from Tennessee, of course had no abolition blood in them.
Well, fall came, and Lincoln was elected; and
although their party was defeated, they seemed
to stick closer to each other than ever before, and
Mary Carter had not yet made a choice. People
used to say she would have to marry them both.
But one day in December Jim came into my
office with his handsome face all aglow, and a
happier and more triumphant light dancing out
of his bright eyes than I ever saw before. I
knew something had happened, but I was struck
all of a heap when he told me that Mary Carter
had promised to marry him; I was so sure it
was Tom she liked best, and I couldn't help
saying, 'But Tom—does he know?' 'Yes, poor
Tom! He says he loved her, but I am sure he
never loved her as I do, and he'll get over it
soon.' After he left I sat musing, and thinking
after all how little we know of a woman's ways,

when who should come in but Tom. His face was downcast and sad, but he tried to cheer up, and when I spoke to him about the matter he said, 'Yes, I am glad Jim has her. I thought she liked me best, but you see I was mistaken, and I would rather he had her than any one else.' I saw he was hit hard, but was trying to be a man, and a generous one, about it, and somehow I couldn't help but think there was a mistake about it all.

"Well, for the rest of that winter times were pretty active and full for me in this little town, for there were a good many people here who afterwards became red-hot Copper-heads, and feeling ran pretty high on all sides. Still, though Mary and the boys were of different political ways of thinking, they all got along finely, and nothing seemed to mar their happiness, and the time was set in spring for Jim's marriage.

"One afternoon late in March the young people of the town to the number of a dozen started down to Elliot's pond for the last skate of the season. I could not go then, but promised to join them in the evening, as it would be moonlight, and they would, besides, light bonfires on the ice near shore. They were to stay out late. It had been pretty warm during the day and the ice had softened a good deal, but towards nightfall it grew cold and froze up tight again. I remember the gloriously beautiful night as though it were yesterday. The moon at its full, the snow—what was left of it— crisp and sparkling under feet, and the sheet of ice glimmering on the pond like a setting of glass.

"As I sauntered down about eight o'clock towards the bridge at the upper end of the pond I heard several screams and shouts for help near by. I rushed down, and there struggling to get up through the ice was Tom Ainsworth, while a rod or two off was Mary Carter entirely help- less. It took me but a moment to break a board off the fence near by and soon have the fellow out, and as he crawled up the bank Mary followed him, very pale and trembling with emotion, and I heard her say something about her darling and that kind of stuff, and the next moment they were kissing each other for all they were worth. I was pretty much astonished, knowing she was engaged to Jim. I stopped that scene by hurrying him off to change his clothes,—I hunted up Jim and put Mary in his charge, and then left without joining the skating party, who were all down at the lower end of the pond a mile away.

"You see I wasn't mistaken after all,—she liked Tom best; and when she saw him, as she thought, drowning, it came all of a sudden to her. In a few days it all came out. Tom was willing to do the honorable thing and go away, but Mary took the matter in her own hands, telling Jim how she felt, and that she never could marry him,—Jim.

"A week after the news of Sumter came to us, and I'll never forget Tom's anguish as he came to my room to tell me the whole story. It seems that what Mary told Jim had changed his entire nature. He cursed both Tom and Mary, told them he would be a living thorn in their sides, threatened all sorts of things, and finally ended by leaving town and going South to join the Confederate army. You cannot imagine his rage unless you knew his character, as I was just beginning to learn it, and he was simply un- shakable once his mind was made up; and this point you must remember because of the sequel.

"Well, those two boys separated never to

meet again till on the battle-field of Iuka, and
then under such strange conditions as war alone
can bring out. Tom enlisted and joined an
Ohio battery, but before going to the front he
was married to Mary. I soon joined the army
as surgeon, and went through the fighting at
Donelson, Henry, Shiloh, the marching and
work during the summer of 1862, and finally
found myself, as I have told you, at Iuka.

" And now to go back to that battle-field where
the two brothers and myself met again. When
Grant had learned of Price's attempt on Iuka,
he ordered Rosecrans with his two divisions of
Hamilton and Stanley to advance on the town
by the roads to the west and south of the town,
while Ord with nine thousand men was to advance on the north. As Rosy had in his two
divisions about nine thousand more, if the whole
eighteen thousand men could all get there at
the same time they could easily hold the place
against Van Dorn and Price together till Grant
had brought up his entire force, if need be.

" Iuka is a beautiful village on the hills, and
to its south just outside the town was the triangular plateau on which the battle took place.
The base of this triangle was north towards the

11*

town, and the point towards the south. The base was about a mile long, but the point lopped off was about a quarter of a mile wide only. Price had fully fourteen thousand men there on the 18th, and he at once caused them to throw up intrenchments on the plateau along the base. Behind them were thick woods, and their position was about as strong as it well could be. Rosecrans did not divide his forces as he was ordered to do, and thus approach by two roads, bringing all his men at once on the field, but scattered them on one road, with Hamilton's division in advance. The skirmishers of this division struck the Confederate pickets about four o'clock on the afternoon of the next day, the 19th, and immediately as fierce a little fight took place as occurred during the entire war. In fact, it is given as a matter of record that no fight had so great a percentage of killed and wounded, for the numbers engaged, as did the battery in Hamilton's division. Look at it, lieutenant, yourself, and you will see as I do that it was one of the most important battles of the war. Ord was far away and did not come up till the next day, when the fight was over; Grant knew nothing of the battle till late that night; while

Rosy came on the battle-field but a moment, and then, not thinking it would be much, went to the rear to hurry up Stanley's troops. So Hamilton's division had to fight the battle alone with but four thousand five hundred men. All depended on them, and to Hamilton alone must belong the entire credit of the victory. It was simply a question of holding his place till night should put an end to the battle, for he knew that if he could do that, then by morning light there would be more than enough troops to take care of all the Johnnies. If he could not hold his ground, then Price would strike Stanley, overthrow him, turn and beat Ord, and thus destroy Grant's army by detail, and all won so far during the war by the Union troops would be lost. Then, making the junction with Van Dorn, the Confederates could have driven Buell over the Ohio and destroyed Grant. So it all depended on Hamilton and his division, and that officer fully realized it, and he fought his men as few officers know how,—always in the front, just when and wherever needed, by his personal example inspiring his men to hold their ground. His horse was killed under him, his clothes perforated with bullets, and every officer

on his staff and body-guard but two either killed
or wounded. But he held his ground for the
three hours of light remaining, and at dark, un-
able to overcome him, the Confederates withdrew, knowing that the next morning Ord and
Rosecrans with the rest of the troops would
be up.

"It was a bloody battle, for we lost over two
hundred and seventy killed and nearly six hundred wounded out of the four thousand five hundred men engaged, while the rebs lost almost
double that out of fourteen thousand men engaged. The key-point of the battle was the
ground held by the Ohio battery, in which Tom
Ainsworth was now a sergeant. It played the
very devil among the rebs, and they determined
to have it. So twice they charged it, but both
times were driven off. Again they formed
columns of attack to storm it, and this time
they came on so there was no stopping them.
The battery did splendid work just then. The
guns seemed alive, so rapidly did they spit out
their showers of grape and canister that tore
great lanes through the approaching masses. I
happened to be near the battery at that time and
saw Tom dismounted, himself aiming and firing

his gun; and, looking over to the rebs, who
should be leading the foremost company of attack but his brother Jim! The very demon was
in Jim's eyes as he recognized Tom, and his face
lighted up with a terrible expression of hate, and
he began, even in that noise and turmoil, to
curse him, when his voice was drowned in an
explosion. Tom had pulled his lanyard, the last
shot fired by the battery, and a shower of grape
went right at Jim's company, which laid out Jim
and half his men. But notwithstanding, the
battery was taken, but soon lost, again taken,
and at last abandoned to our men at night-fall.

"Well, that is all about the fight. Hamilton,
I think, is the man to whom all the credit is due,
as Rosecrans was nowhere about. That night
the rebs left in such a hurry that we had to bury
their dead and take care of their wounded. I
had my hands full, for I was short of assistants.
I had ordered a house in town seized and turned
into a hospital. It had belonged to a Confederate general officer, and was one of the largest
and finest houses in the village, and surrounded
by a beautiful shaded lawn. When the house
was filled with wounded, and there were still
many more coming, I directed a number to be

i

placed outside on the lawn under the shade of
trees.   As there they had plenty of fresh air,
not cold at that time of the year, they were
really as comfortable as in the house.

"Towards evening of the second day after the
battle I got my first chance for a little rest, and,
taking my pipe and a camp-stool, I went out on
the lawn to have a quiet smoke.   I sat down as
far from the groups of wounded as I well could,
though they were so many that was not saying
much.   At my feet a little way from me was the
apparently lifeless body of a Confederate who
had been brought in severely wounded, but had
died, as was supposed, before the surgeons could
get around to him, and the burial-parties were
still busy with our own men.   Part of his skull
had been torn off by a piece of grape-shot or a
shell, and the brain or part of it was protruding
in a bulbous balloon-shaped mass, confined, it
seemed, by a thin tissue.   Although covered
with blood and dirt, there was something about
him that struck my attention, and, bending over
him, I discovered it was poor Jim Ainsworth.
At first I was glad that he was done for, for I
knew he must have been instantly killed, and
Tom and his wife could henceforth live in peace.

But even while looking at him, it seemed to me that there was the very slightest respiration, and to my surprise I found on examination that there was. 'Impossible,' I said to myself, and I knelt down to watch the closer. A man with the top of his head blown off, the brain protruding, left in the open air for forty-eight hours without attention,—why, such a thing was never heard of. But my senses to the contrary notwithstanding, this man was actually still alive. I took out my watch and counted the respirations, and then set about to help him what little I could, for I felt certain he would die very soon. So, as death was certain, I took from my pocket-case of instruments a small sharp knife and sliced off the protruding part of the brain, and then plastered the skin over the hole in the skull as well as I could. But he still continued to live even after that, and so I injected into him stimulants; and to my great astonishment the number of respirations soon increased and seemed stronger.

"Here was a case to delight any professional man, and perhaps I might be able to keep life in him for a long enough time for his people to come to him. I sent for Tom, and he came the next day. To my unbounded delight, after setting up a tent over the patient and injecting nourishment into him, he seemed to grow stronger, and the idea occurred to me that he might live. From that time the attention of all the surgeons was placed on Jim, and with every care and Tom as a nurse, to make a long story short, he did pull through, though it took some months to do it. Tom could only stay for two weeks, but he knew Jim would live before the end of his furlough.

"I went back to Memphis that fall, and had Jim brought there and put under my especial care in one of our hospitals. Tom joined his battery, and it was not long ere I heard of his promotion. Poor fellow, he was killed at Vicksburg the next year, and Mary was left a widow with one little child.

"Now for the curious part of the story. I thought, of course, that as Jim recovered he would at least remain an idiot for the rest of his life, and certainly would remember no one nor any of his past life. Not much. He not only knew me, but his mind seemed as bright and clear as formerly, except on one point alone. He asked after Tom and Mary and the old acquaintances up here; he talked of the war, of old times; he cursed the Union cause till I ordered him to be quiet while in a Union hospital and living at the expense of the Government and men who had saved his life. But in all his talk of Tom and Mary there was never the slightest malice or bitterness, or reference to the old feud and trouble. At first I thought he wished to avoid the subject, but I soon became convinced it was actually not in his head, and therefore, speaking of it myself to him, I became convinced it was all a blank to him. In other words, what had been the most exciting topic of his life was now a perfect blank. If you ask me how I account for it, I tell you I cannot. Men have often lived days, even years, with bullets and pieces of metal in their brains, but I never heard of a case where a man lived with part of his brain cut or blown away. But he did, and whether or not that part of the brain that I sliced off contained the memory of his love and hate for Mary and Tom is a mystery to me. In every other respect he was himself, and the next spring, when he was exchanged with a number of prisoners, he went off cursing the Union cause and with no thanks for the men who had saved him, but with loving messages for Tom and Mary. He never saw Tom, but was killed towards the close of the war in a little skirmish by a bullet, this time in the brain that was left him. He had then attained the rank of colonel.

"Yes, lieutenant, I've seen many strange wounds, but, take it all in all, that one reached the top notch of them all. I've often wished he might have lived, as then he might have taken poor Tom's place, though that is doubtful, as Mary Ainsworth has had many offers since then, but has always remained faithful to Tom's memory. If this was a story from a novel, and not a true tale, he would have lived and married Mary."

THE STORY OF ALCATRAZ.

135

"Four cards, Doc? You are playing rather a reckless game to-night. Better pull out and lose a little than risk all you've got on a single card. Nearly a thousand in that pot, though,—don't blame you much for staying. Lord, you've got a nerve!"

As the cards fell, Paul Durmier turned the corners up stealthily, sheltering them with his hand from the eyes of the other players. A king—another—an ace—a king. When a man's last dollar is in the banker's pocket, and his last chip in the jack-pot, such a draw is providential. The hand stood three kings and two aces. He was too skillful a gambler to allow the fire of joy which had sprung up in his heart to warm the lines of his countenance.

"Steady, gentlemen," he said, quietly; "I think we'll fatten that a little before proceeding. There's my check for five hundred dollars. No doubt you'll all come right in." Then, softly to himself, he added, "I don't bet with Government money except on a sure thing. When a king full is not good, I'll go bankrupt."

There was a stir among the players, and some one grumbled about "bluffing." Four of them laid down their hands, shook their heads, and looked at one another. A gentleman in black, sitting opposite, turned his cards cautiously, faced them on the table, drew forth a check-book and wrote. His heavy brows covered the twinkle in his little beady eyes, and a furtive smile played at the corners of his mouth under the seclusion of his waxed moustache.

"I'll see that five and raise it five, Dr. Durmier," he said, coldly. "The gentlemen know that my check on the Bank of California is worth what it is written for."

Four deep breaths issued from the lungs of the vanquished players. They tipped back their chairs and looked at one another aghast, as if they had just seen a man fall from the roof of a building. Such wagers were not ordinarily laid in the quiet rooms of the Bavarian Club. It was against the rules; it was contrary to precedent. They watched the Doctor write the duplicate of his former check,—five hundred dollars on the Pacific National. The issue was reached.

' "Anything to please you, Mr. Jerome. I'll risk that to look at your hand." The players bent forward eagerly. The gentleman with the waxed moustache turned his cards carefully and spread them out in plain view.

Four queens and an ace!

Dr. Durmier rose to his feet, leaned upon the table, and stared at them wildly. There was no doubt. He had gambled away a thousand dollars of the public funds.

It was a climax that others had reached before, but never so quickly. It usually takes months to pile up a deficit of a thousand dollars. He had accomplished the feat in less than ten minutes,—surely a damnable distinction. Reeling through the open door, he staggered down the stairway to the coat-room, stubbornly striving to appear indifferent. Some one led him to the bar and placed a glass of whisky in his hand.

"Drink that, old man; you need a bracer," urged the Samaritan.

He pushed it nervously away. "No, no; I am only tired of playing. The boat leaves in half an hour,—good-by!" Rushing down the stairway, he pushed open the heavy doors fiercely and disappeared.

Half an hour later, just as the whistle of the little steamer was blowing for the midnight trip around the harbor, he staggered down the gangplank.

* * * * * *

Later still he stood behind the granite battlement that crowns the citadel of Alcatraz, and looked out over the dark still waters of the bay. The footsteps of the sentinels were stifled in the stillness of the night; the last belated tug had sought the wharf; the last glimmering light of the city had faded in the mist that overhung the lower bay. The strong rays from Alcatraz light-house, sweeping out through the Golden Gate, mingled with the darting flashes from Fort Point and Bonita, and hurried on to warn the sleepy midnight watch of the narrowing, cliff-bound straits. Nature slept, and softly breathed amid the monotonous rushes of the surf against the feet of the rocks.

Far down below him the lighter objects of the Island peered upward like spectres out of the darkness,—the winding road descending to the dock, the stone tennis court, the white walls of the light-house, the bronze figures of the field-guns. By a side glance he could detect the outlines of the flower-beds, with the gravel walks between, and their heavy border of solid shot. He could see the bells of the calla lilies, the voluptuous velvet of the Jacque roses, and the hanging jewels of the century plant rising in the centre of the garden.

Never before, even in the summer twilight, when every object in nature forces itself on the eye more vividly than the central figure in a painting,—never before had the homely images of the Rock impressed themselves so sharply upon his mind. His eye flitted restlessly from one object to another, seeking one whose diffidence forbade its intrusion on his self-sought solitude.

There was the little adjutant's office perching like a martin's nest on the edge of the cliff, with the tall light-house standing over it like an Arab sentinel clad in white. Lower down the winding road, like a trio of mastiffs sleeping with one eye open, reposed the commanding officer's quarters, with its two flanking companions, the captains' quarters. Still lower, on the first terrace, rose the great gray hospital; and below it the rambling masses of the prison buildings were lost in the vague shadows that encircled the water's edge.

The peace that dwelt upon the face of slumbering nature contrasted painfully with the tempest of emotions that swelled the heart of Paul Durmier. Anguish, regret, unspeakable dread, lashed the rock of reason like angry waters. In the sparkling dome above him seemed to swing the arms of a great balance—to be or not to be. Here in the open night might Fate cast the final atom which would launch him forward to the unexplored beyond.

Such heart strains and such perplexity could not be borne long. There was a pain at his heart. Shadowy images were floating before his eyes, and a dullness filled his brain and seemed to crush his senses. Other men had done this thing, and naught could spare them. They fled to other countries, dishonored, ruined. It would be better to die than endure dishonor. The Government trusts no one, yet it crushes whom it cannot trust. The thought turned his brain to fire.

Then the dear wife—the little boy. They must not know; they could never bear his guilt. When life is dishonor, death is—but reason stops at the bounds of life. No one can tell of the life whose birth is death. The pain that galls eternal dissolution would be rest compared with the agony of living shame. The dread of the hereafter is not more terrible than the dread of existence cursed by the scorn of men.

But there was hope. If by any possibility the soul should not be immortal, the end of all things is in death, Life and honor might be made to terminate in the same breath. Immortality might be only a fiction—a mere philosopher's fancy. There was hope in the thought.

He turned and straightened, questioning the horizon with his sharp eyes. Only the darkness answered. Shapeless masses of shadow slumbered under the dark outline of Tamalpais. The demon eyes of the Golden Gate gleamed with a melancholy radiance. Nature turned her face from the guilt that blackened his soul.

With noiseless steps he returned along the plank walk of the sentry's gallery, passing down the iron stairway and through the western barbican. Choosing the stone pavement, so that his footsteps would not grate upon the gravel, he stole silently down towards his office. There were some minor official matters that would need attention. As he paused at the head of

the stone stairway which descended to the first
terrace, he glanced upward and saw the portly
light-house keeper trimming the lamps in the
lens gallery. It was the end of the midnight
watch. He crept on to the office and turned up
the lamp at his desk. The attendant sleeping
in the adjoining room would not wake before
reveille for anything less than an earthquake.
Rapidly he turned over his papers, balanced his
accounts, signed checks for the cash in bank,
and closed the books. When all was complete
he gathered them together and fastened them
with a rubber band. That closed his business
with the Government, his erstwhile friend, his
present enemy.

Dipping his pen, he again wrote upon a slip
of paper, "Take care of little Walley," and
pinned a check to it. Mechanically his hand
began to trace characters upon the tablet before
him. "To die is the end of all. It blots out
existence. The elements of life return to earth.
Death is the end of growth—it is the end of
life—there is nothing more."

The sentinel's cry at the prison bridge warned
, him of the passing hours. Already it was
morning. He arranged the papers on the table,

threw the scribblings into the waste-basket, and turned down the lamp. The glow of morn was rising over Mount Diablo. He ascended the carriage road and climbed the stone stairway.

Entering the door of the bastion over which the flag waves, in the first room he came upon his study desk, and on it the scattered manuscript of his book. How long, how earnestly, he had labored for its completion, trying to stifle the gaming passion under the strain of mental effort! He had worked until his head was filled with pains, and fiery images floated before his eyes. Thank God, now that it was finished it was a work to be proud of. He sat down, and on the first page of the manuscript wrote, " This is for Walley."

There was light enough now to render objects in the room visible, so he turned out the lamp. Up-stairs his wife might be awake. In order that he might not disturb her, he removed his shoes. Every dainty object in the room made him think tenderly of her,—the silken cigarcase, the embroidered slipper-holder, the pictures hanging upon the wall. Poor little woman, how unworthy he felt now of her pure love.

The evil passion which had blighted his life showed only more blackly by contrast with her wifely devotion.

It was time to arouse: the morning was fast breaking—in the basement the Chinese servant was kindling the fires.

His hunting-coat hung in the closet. Hesitatingly, cautiously, he drew from the pocket a loaded shell. Would he take another? No; the thought was cruel. But death is the end of all, and to die in youth and happiness is better than to live and drink the bitter cup of dishonored widowhood. He took another shell, opened the breech of the gun, and inserted it in the barrel. Farewell home and the happy days and the friends that come and go. Farewell life that is not so lovely, after all.

He threw off his coat and vest and with cat-like tread ascended the stairs. In the first room was the baby sleeping in his crib. Poor little fellow! He would never know, and he would not be happier if he did. He bent and kissed the curly brow. The door of his wife's room stood ajar. He entered and closed it softly. She lay there smiling in her sleep, her arms above her head, the light of the morning sun

wreathing her in its warm embrace. How pure,
how womanly she looked! Oh, what cruel fate
should doom a holy life to end so rudely! He
threw back the covering. She did not move.
The abdomen was sudden, fatal, and accessible.
He reached over the foot-board and placed the
muzzle of the gun within an inch of her cloth-
ing. Would not the officer in the adjoining
room hear the report? No: he had passed the
night at the Presidio. He pulled the trigger.
Only a tremor passed over the slender form.
The peaceful smile was fixed immovably. The
room was filling with smoke, for the sheets had
caught fire from the flame of the discharge.
Reaching over, with his hands he crushed the
fire from the blazing cloth. How fortunate it is
that instant death prevents the flow of blood!

Now his turn had come, and he welcomed
it. He drew forth the empty shell, inserted
the second charge, and cocked the hammer.
Which was the easiest way? How would he
manage? Easily enough. He inclined the
muzzle towards him and pressed his body
against it. Then balancing himself upon one
foot he reached forward with the toe of the
other and touched the trigger. A report—a

cloud of smoke—a heavy fall—and the shadow
of a great doubt was made a lucid certainty.

Ah Wong was waiting in the basement below
in great desperation. The breakfast would keep
no longer. Surely his master and mistress had
been keeping late hours. They did not usually
slumber until ten o'clock. He would steal softly
up the stairway and see if they were yet awake.
Perhaps they were dressing,—he would not show
impatience by calling them. On the way he met
the fat light-house keeper standing in the open
doorway holding a basket.

"How do! What you catchee?" asked Wong
in his usual monotone.

"Some eggs for your mistress. What! Not
up yet?"

"No, cap. Me call 'em now."

The light-keeper waddled back to the light-
house, and ·Wong continued his ascent. He
opened the door of the baby's room and peered
in cautiously. Walley was crowing and kicking
his heels in the air. Wong stole over to the
crib and tickled him.

"What's mattah? You no get hungry yet?"
he asked.

He rapped at the door of the adjoining room.

No answer. He rapped again quite loud. Were they ill? Perhaps they had remained in the city the night before. He turned the knob and softly pushed the door ajar. What a queer smell! He poked his little shaven head through, and started back as if struck by an unseen hand.

Down the stairs he flew, leaving his wooden shoes tumbling along behind him; then running barefooted into the adjoining quarters he besought a lieutenant in terror-stricken tones to come quickly.

"Plenty devils,—him very sick on floor!" he cried, pointing upward.

Other officers joined the lieutenant, and together they ascended the stairs. An odor of burned powder pervaded the air. They pushed open the door and saw—that the army would have a promotion and a double funeral. Both bodies were cold and stiff.

On the floor lay the young surgeon, the blood slowly oozing from an ugly, blackened wound. At his feet the double-barreled shot-gun, falling, had jarred open at the breech. An empty shell was in the gun, another on the floor. On the bed lay the white form of the girl wife, her arms above her head, resting on the dark masses of

13*

her hair. It was as if she slept and was smiling in her sleep. They threw sheets over the bodies and drew painfully away. Before any friendly hand could interpose, the civil law relating to sudden death must be complied with.

Sorrow came and dwelt upon the summit of the Rock. The wise coroners appeared, and, shaking their heads, said, solemnly, "Murder and suicide during an attack of temporary insanity." Insanity has always played second to murder.

When friends came to lay their last offering of flowers, they found the two lying side by side in the little parlor under the flag. Choking down a sob, they looked into the white faces and said, "Who would have thought—so young —poor things."

They made a single grave under the cypress-trees in the great cemetery back of the Presidio, and there one sunny morning the little steamer bore them, still lying side by side, on its deck. There was a procession that followed slowly up the hill, there were many mourners, there were prayers that were thoughtful and sincere, and tears fell to the earth that day which were tender and full of love. The words of the minister were comforting, for no one knew but the coroner was right, and no one thought of the deadly purpose which commits a crime.

The dwellers on the Rock to-day show you a vacant bastion that was long since abandoned to the bats and evil spirits. Some say that at midnight you can see lights flitting past the windows. But only one will offer to tell you the story of the bloody deed committed there, and that is the portly light-house keeper. He dwells with pride upon each detail, and claims the honor of being first to view the dead, and to convey the news of the fearful event to the daily newspapers. Yet even he, when he reads this narrative, may learn that coroners can err, and insanity be not always connected with murder.

THE OTHER FELLOW.

THE OTHER FELLOW.

OUR nearest neighbor was Mr. John Deve-reux, of Coramballa Station, seventy-eight miles away,—tolerably close as things went in the Queensland "back blocks" in those days. He took up a block of country next to my brothers in the latter part of '85 and stocked it with sheep. Shortly after his arrival, I rode over from We-aldiwindi—my brothers' station—to pay my respects. I found a tall, bronzed, bearded man, apparently about thirty-two years of age, who greeted me with perfect politeness, yet with such chilling reserve that the prospect of a future close acquaintance appeared rather remote.

Nothing daunted by this reception, I paid several visits to Coramballa during the next few months. I was always received with that hospitality which is a canon of bush etiquette, still, I fancied that Devereux, in his heart, wished I would stay away.

You meet all kinds of queer characters in the bush. There being no public opinion to con-

sider, the mask of conventionality is often cast
aside and hidden traits in a man's character become his marked characteristics. But a neighbor is a neighbor even though he be surly as a
grizzly bear; in fact, you are glad to have one
of any kind in the "back blocks." So, not in
the least deterred by the continued frigidity
with which my friendly advances were met, I
made my visits more frequent in the hope of
some day inducing my surly neighbor to "come
out of his shell." The opinion I formed of
Devereux was that this gloomy reserve was not
his natural bent, but was simply a misanthropic
humor engendered by some overwhelming disappointment in earlier life. I felt sure that beneath his distant manner and semi-morose dis-
position there lay a warm and generous nature.
In the end my perseverance was rewarded by a
measure of success. While Devereux never at
any time manifested any warmth in his greet-
ings, he so far relaxed from his former distant
bearing as to accord me the ghost of a welcom-
ing smile when he shook hands. I looked upon
this as proof positive of the correctness of my
theory, and accepted it as an indication that my
visits were no longer deemed unwelcome.

I had no financial interest—I am sorry to say —in my brothers' property, but, Micawber-like, was simply waiting there "for something to turn up." So, having no call upon my time, I was enabled to spend more of my leisure at Coramballa than at Wealdiwindi.

I am bound to confess that I felt not a little curiosity in regard to the past life of my taciturn friend. He, however, rarely spoke of it, and then only in such a casual way as to afford no foundation for anything but mere conjecture.

I learned to like Devereux very much, and began to hope that the sentiment was mutual, as indeed it proved to be, for we afterwards became very warm friends.

He had been at Coramballa nine months or so when some lady cousins braved the solitudes of the bush and paid us a visit at Wealdiwindi. Devereux had never been to our station, and thinking this a good opportunity to "draw him out," I rode over to invite him to spend a week or two with us. He listened to me, and then quietly and politely declined the invitation. Noticing my look of chagrin, he said, in an apologetic tone,—

"You perhaps think me a boor in declining your hospitality, but I came out to this sparsely-settled country expressly to avoid society of any kind. I do not wish to appear churlish, and though, believe me, I value your friendship very highly, I cannot make any exception to what is now the rule of my life, even for you. But come in and take something to drink."

We sat down in the front room: Devereux mixed a couple of glasses of grog and filled his pipe. He smoked in silence awhile as if considering something. Then he laid his pipe aside, got up and took a photograph from a bracket on the wall. He handed it to me, and said, abruptly,—

"Do you recognize that?" It was the picture of a bright, smiling, manly-looking young fellow of some one or two and twenty. There was an expression about the eyes that reminded me somewhat of his own; but when I looked at his bronzed, heavily-bearded face, and again at the picture of the laughing young fellow, hairless save for a small curling moustache, the semblance seemed to vanish.

"I can't say I do," I replied, after looking at the photograph for some moments. "I don't think it is any one I have seen before. Is it a brother of yours?"

"No," said Devereux, with a peculiar sad smile. "He was not a brother of mine." Again he smoked awhile in silence, and I looked at the picture, wondering whether it was a link in the chain of his past.

"No," he repeated, musingly. "He was not a brother of mine, though ten years ago we were alike as two peas. If it will not bore you, I will tell you an episode in his life."

"Fire away!" said I, filled with astonishment at the idea of his telling a story: he had barely uttered twenty consecutive words during our nine months' acquaintance.

He laid down his pipe, took a sip at his grog, and began,—

"With Jack's,—I need not give you his other name, every one called him Jack,—with Jack's early youth we have nothing to do. It will be sufficient for me to say that at the usual age he went to Rugby, where he was somewhat of a 'dab' at cricket and foot-ball. After several years of floundering among Greek roots and algebraic formulæ at that ancient seat of juvenile learning, he somehow managed to scuffle into Sandhurst, and in due time got a commission. While at Sandhurst, Jack, who was a romantic, susceptible fellow, became acquainted with the daughter of a half-pay officer who lived in that vicinity.

"She was one of the prettiest girls I ever saw. Such eyes, such hair, and such a figure, and withal of gentle, loving nature. No wonder Jack lost his heart. I said Jack lost his heart. I should rather have said he fell madly in love with her, for, if there is such a passion as the love poets dream of and novelists rave about, Jack experienced it in all its Ouidaesque intensity.

"He was two and twenty then,—just the age when the boyish heart is most prone to such weaknesses. And Claire—Claire Tempest was her name—loved Jack,—at least she said she did,—and Jack was just the happiest, brightest fellow in the world.

"Jack was poor,—poor as a church mouse. He had, in fact, nothing but his commission; and you probably know what a miserable dog an officer is in the British army who has no private fortune. And Claire's prospects were not much brighter, her father having only a limited income outside of his half-pay. But, then, they loved each other, these two, and in that blissful knowledge they spent a happy year exchanging vows, altogether regardless of the cold logic of finance. Then Jack asked the general for Claire's hand, whereat the old soldier stormed and swore, called Jack a 'damned, presumptuous young pauper,' and threatened to kick him out of the house if he ever mentioned or thought of such a thing again.

"Jack was bound to admit that he was a pauper,—his worldly possessions amounted to something less than seven hundred pounds; but he thought the old general might have expressed his opinion in more euphemistic language.

"So Jack talked the matter over with Claire, and they came to the conclusion that they could not marry on his pay. Would she wait? Claire kissed him, and with love's sweet hyperbole said she would wait a hundred years for 'her Jack.'

"And Jack, looking at the subject from all its bearings, decided that there was nothing for it but to emigrate.

"'Far pastures are always green,' you know,

l   14*

and after a great deal of looking over pamphlets and other printed matter eulogistic of colonial advantages, he decided upon South Africa as his future home. 'There's gold and diamonds out there,' he argued to himself with boyish enthusiasm; 'and I have youth, and health, and strength, and seven hundred pounds, and I must succeed.'

"He took a couple of months' leave before resigning and went down to visit some relatives in the west of England. During his absence, Claire was introduced to a Mr. Forester, some London financial swell, a fellow with heaps of tin, stocks, and bonds, and all that sort of thing, and an office on Lombard Street. He paid Claire marked attention, and visited the general's house so frequently, and took Claire to balls and operas and all that kind of thing, that people began to say they were engaged.

"Jack heard of this in some way, and, of course, being deeply in love, became insanely jealous. He came back post-haste. His first question after the usual lovers' greeting was,—

" 'What is all this about this banker fellow?'

" 'Why, Jack, what do you mean? which banker fellow?' Claire asked, innocently.

" 'Which banker fellow?' blurted Jack, fiercely. 'Why, the banker fellow,—the fellow from London.'

" 'Oh!' smiled Claire, 'Mr. Forester. Why, Jack, you silly, jealous boy, he is fifty,—old enough to be my father twice over.'

" 'And you don't care a rap for him,—and,— and it's not true what people say?' gulped Jack.

" And then Claire nestled close to him and said,—

" 'Oh, Jack, my own darling Jack, how could you think it,' and held up her pretty face to be kissed, and of course Jack kissed it, believed her, and was happy again.

" Well, the time came for him to leave. The old general was so glad to get him out of the way that he yielded to Claire's entreaties, and took her down to Southampton to see Jack off.

" Jack lingered at the gangway at the imminent risk of missing the steamer, and, at the final moment, strained Claire to his breast in a last fond embrace, while she repeated for the hundredth time a tearful promise to wait for and think of him always.

" Jack stood at the stern, gazing at the receding shore with misty eyes, until the slender figure waving the last good-by was lost in the blur of distance.

"Poor Jack! How bravely he tried during the voyage to be his old genial self. If he had not felt Claire to be the most loving, trustful, faithful girl in all the world, I believe he would have been tempted to go back; but he had every faith in her constancy, and he felt that he must brave this separation a few years for her sake.

"At the Cape he tried everything that a 'new chum' with limited means usually does. He 'dabbled' in wool, in cattle, and in mining shares, and while he met with varying success, as the old bush song says, he

'. . . did no good at all, as a rule.'

"But Jack was stout-hearted and hopeful and had no doubt of ultimate success. He wrote cheering letters, to which, in due time, loving answers came. Suddenly, however, these answers ceased, and when week after week passed, and no replies came to his letters, he grew despondent and gloomy.

"'She could not have forgotten him so soon.' Either she was ill or her father intercepted his letters. There was something wrong, but it was not with her. He would have staked his soul on her faith and love. And then he would write another letter.

"About this time the trouble with the Basutos began. The organization of the Mounted Rifles appealed to Jack's soldier instincts, and he resolved to join them. He invested his remaining capital in some mining shares, and enlisted. His former military training here stood him in good stead, and promotion came rapidly. Jack's low spirits revived under the excitement of the times, and he was once more his old genial self.

"Well, I'm getting rather long-winded, am I not? So I'll cut it short. Those niggers gave us lots of work, and on several occasions made things rather lively for us. One day we met them in force, and for a time matters went against us. A whole lot of them were sheltered in a belt of scrub on our right, from which they picked us off at their leisure. Mind you, these were no naked assegai-throwing savages, but fellows who were armed as well as we were, and no mean marksmen, either.

"'If we only had a mountain howitzer,' sighed the colonel, 'I'd make it hot for those black devils. But we haven't, so it's got to be done some other way.'

"' Captain Travers,' he said to the captain of Jack's troop, ' take your troop and clean those beggars out.'

"Travers saluted and formed the troop for the duty assigned him. Many a stout fellow's heart came into his mouth, for there would be a score of empty saddles when the troop came back, if, indeed, it ever came back at all. Travers rode at the scrub, and soon men began to fall. Half-way over, Travers wavered. He had lost his lieutenant and twelve men already, and the troop was only three-quarters strong. As he turned in the saddle to shout some order, a bullet struck him in the temple and he fell from his horse. Instantly, Jack—he was troop sergeant-major—rode to the front. ' Follow me, boys,' he shouted, ' I command this troop now.' And his stentorian ' Charge!' met with a wild, responsive hurrah from the men. His enthusiasm aroused their flagging spirits and filled them with all their old dash and vim.

"Well, we cleaned those niggers out completely, but Jack was brought back with a hole in his shoulder, and invalided to the rear. His wound turned out to be more serious than at first supposed, the ball having passed perilously close to a main artery. The doctor looked grave, and said that Jack had a chance, but that it wasn't worth much. And, indeed, it was touch and go with him for days. But when he began to mend, there was good news for him. A letter from Capetown informed him that, owing to some remarkably rich 'finds,' his mining shares had been sold at a large profit, and that something like ten thousand pounds lay to his credit in the Bank of Africa, at Capetown.

"This news gave him new heart. The tide had turned, luck was his at last. The thought filled his feeble frame with a glow of ecstacy. Ten thousand pounds would buy a handsome property in South Africa, and as soon as he was able he would go over to England and bring her out. But he might die. He was yet pale and feeble, with but a frail hold on life. He would secure his little fortune to her in case anything *should* happen to him. So that evening he sent for a lawyer to make his will, and when he had appended a faint scrawl to it by way of signature, he went to sleep with hope and love in his heart.

"A week or so later the English mail was

due. I remember the day very well. It was a calm, still morning, and the sun shone in through the open window, making the plain, whitewashed room look quite bright and cheery. Jack lay near the window, looking for the hoisting of the flag on the Government building that announced the arrival of the mail.

" It was a long time since he had had a letter. How anxiously he had awaited the arrival of every mail, and how confidently he had expected that when one failed the next would surely bring him news.

" He watched the distribution of the letters in the ward with hungry eyes. Sure enough, there was a letter for him, and from Claire, too. How his heart leaped when he saw it. He opened it with trembling fingers, and then uttered a strange gulping sound that brought the nurses quickly to his side. At first they thought this sudden shock was death. But he had only swooned, and beside him on the coverlet lay the cause,—the delicately perfumed note from Claire.

" Well, perhaps she only did what nine women out of ten would have done, and no doubt was congratulated by her friends on having taken a very sensible course.

"And Jack? No, he did not die. But that letter killed all faith and hope and belief within him. It filled his heart with gall and wormwood, and made him a cynic, a misanthrope, a hermit, if you will.

"What was in the note? It is so long ago now that I can't recall the exact words. But it ran somehow like this,—

"'DEAR JACK,—All your letters have been received. The last one touched me so I had to write and tell you. It was foolish of us to care for each other, Jack. I was poor and you were poorer; why then should we waste the best years of our lives in waiting for that which could never be. Poor people have no right to fall in love. Good-by, Jack; if you ever cared for me, forgive me, and in time you will forget.'

"It was signed Claire Forester. She had married the banker, and,—and,—well, that is all."

"And what became of the other fellow,—of Jack?" I asked.

"Oh!" said Devereux, calmly, as he refilled his pipe, "I am the other fellow."

BUTTONS.

BUTTONS.

I.

"EYES" the girls called him. Well might they have sung,—

> " And when your glances rest on me,
>   Right here they make me feel so funny."

The class called him " Shanks," for he was *very* long, and to see him in the riding-hall with those legs of his clasping the bare ribs of a Roman-nosed brute that had broken the head of nearly every other man that had tried to ride him, was a sight for gods and men. At least Tommy Dobbs thought so, but then to little Tommy " Shanks" was perfection.

It was at the " Graduation Hop;" the emancipated sure-of-diplomas had resolved to let their moustaches grow, and, with the energies that remained, assisted by Strauss and Waldteufel, to waltz into the hearts of all the pretty girls in the room. All of them—the girls—were eager to dance with " Eyes," and many a heart flut-

tered as the tall, graceful cadet bowed and
begged for the pleasure, *et cætera.* Yet he
chose to dance oftener with Miss Daisy Van
Stump than with any of the others, and as the
twain glided noiselessly over the glassy floor,
many another pair paused to admire what
seemed to be the poetic embodiment of the
melody the band was playing.

But even waltzes must have an end, and as
the "voluptuous swell" ceased, "Eyes" and his
fair partner strolled away from the room, out
upon the green and towards the Hudson, whose
calm waters reflected the twinkling of the myr-
iads of stars that shone in the cloudless blue
above.

"And so you go away to-morrow, Miss
Daisy?"

"Yes; in the morning."

"Then I may not see you. I am *so* sorry——"

"So am I,—we go to the Springs,—but we
shall see you in New York? We return in
September; and, Mr. Eyes,—I beg pardon,
Mr.——"

"No, no; call me 'Eyes,' Miss Daisy. Ah!
Daisy, if I may speak——"

There! I can't go on. There is but one

language for this sort of thing, and as all of us have been in love at least once, it is hardly necessary to encumber the record with what would be simply a rehearsal of what has been going on ever since Adam and Eve began it. Ill-natured people say that Eve began it. Well, I'm glad she did. Perhaps Adam was——

But let us get back to our pair of rapt ones.

There was moonlight all about them, music filled the air, and flowers bloomed amid the love that stirred their hearts. Why say more? Stay! Yes: as they re-entered the room it was observed in a stage whisper by the eldest Miss Sternchase, who had been at the Point every season since the Mexican war, that a button was missing from the left breast of "Eyes's" jacket, and that one of the pale-blue satin lozenges that adorned Miss Daisy's gown was not where the eldest Miss Sternchase had last seen it.

The next afternoon many people stood on the wharf waiting for the steamer which was to carry them away. The Van Stump family— father, mother, and Daisy—were of the number, and the crowd was freckled here and there with youthful *militaires*,—some going away, many saying the last few words they would ever speak to the pink ears that listened; that had listened to others the year before; whose owners would be ready the coming summer to accept the devotion of the next graduating class. But Miss Daisy was not one of these light-hearted triflers, —at least as far as "Eyes" was concerned; and he, too, was there, looking as if, but for the bystanders and Van Stump *père et mère*, he would have taken her in his arms and kept her there forever. But he couldn't.

Van Stump *père* was said to be "made of money," and he looked it. The *mère* was fat, forty, and very red. People said that while her husband furnished the money, all the "blood" was on her side. Miss Daisy was a darling. How she became possessed of such parents—I mean as to looks—Mr. Darwin might have explained. I can't. She was tall,—not too tall,—a figure round, yet lithe and springy, with violet eyes and hair of wavy chestnut; a face that was grave when in repose, and that flashed like a sudden burst of sunshine when she smiled; and she had that "excellent thing,"—a voice that was "*ever* soft, gentle, and low."

So "Eyes" had to content himself with the barest of partings,—a throbbing grasp; a yearn-

ing look; a tremulous "good-by;" a whispered
"God bless you!" Then "all aboard!" was
sung out. The boat moved into mid-stream,
leaving poor "Eyes" on the pier to watch with
all his soul the fast-receding face and form of
what was all the world to him.

He had actually forgotten that a Being with a
tape-measure was waiting at the other end of
the road to take his measure for a uniform!
And as he walked quickly up the hill, little
Dobbs, very much out of breath, overtook him.

"Hallo, Shanks, old boy! What'll you give
for some news? I've seen the list. You and I
get the —th Cavalry,—think of it! So we may
as well go out together."

"Congratulate you, Chick," was the reply.'

"Chick" was the fond abbreviation of Chiquito, as Tommy was styled by the class "for
short," somebody said.

Shanks had naturally asked for a cavalry regiment, but how Chick had managed to climb into
the saddle was not patent to the rest of the class,
who knew his capacity for tumbling head-first
into the tan-bark whenever his steed—and all
the horses in the riding-hall were acquainted
with Tommy—grew tired of drill. There was

m

but one solution,—he had used family influence (for he came from the whisky part of Kentucky) to claim such an assignment in order to be near his dearest friend.

It was arranged, then, that "the twins," as they were sometimes called, should start in company for Dakota, on whose wide plains their regiment was fast forgetting all about civilization.

"And now," said Chick, "what are you going to do with yourself? I must go home, of course; but, hang it! I don't want to stay in that distillery-soaked country too long, and shall get to the seaside as soon as a decent regard for the bones of my ancestors will permit."

"To say the truth, Chick, I hardly know; my guardian's people expect me to spend part of the next three months with them; but I shall run away down to the sea, and take a good long look at it, for you and I, dear boy, are not likely to see much salt-water in the next few years. Where do you bring up?"

"Oh, I shall go to that place where they have a lot of rocks and sand, and fish and things. Somewhere in Maine,—hang it! I can't think of the name. I've had to remember such a lot of stuff about HO^2, and all the rest of it (*so* useful in the cavalry), that hang me if I can recollect anything that I *do* want to know. But it begins with a B and has a pool, whatever that is."

" Chick, my boy, that's just where I'm going, —Biddeford Pool. Meet me there. Let's see, —I must go to Richfield in——"

" Yes; I know. *She* will be there. Go on. Congratulate you, old fellow, and all that; lots of tin, and as for beauty——" Here Chick clasped his hands and gazed at the sky.

" Don't be a donkey, Dobbs. I shall be there" (severely)—" at Biddeford in August."

" Pardon me. But, Shanks, dear old fellow, I saw it all when you both came back to the ball-room last night, and—Gad! I'm as happy about it as if—as if—as if I were going to marry you myself!"

By this time the two friends had reached the hallowed spot where the Being from New York was waiting with the tape-measure. One of the results of his efforts was rather startling to Tommy's mamma, who said, when her son appeared to her wondering eyes in the full-dress uniform of a second lieutenant of cavalry,

"Sakes alive, Tommy! if you don't look jest like the inside of a mustard-pot!"

II.

The harvest moon in the fullness thereof was making a very early start just above the eastern horizon, glinting with a rosy red the jagged rocks that make picturesque the southwest coast of Maine, and in the mellow light it cast along the glistening beach many pairs of human doves found food for tender words. But of these, two only are just now very interesting.

Who were they?

Listen.

"What a delightful night for boating, is it not?" This from one who at first glance looked very like the Daisy.

But she wasn't *The.* And yet her likeness to Daisy was the cause of the interest, the something, that, as it overhung the tender edge of friendship, was felt for her by her companion, who answered,—

"Yes; look how the light seems to swim upon the waves. How calm it is!"

A pudgy youth who was the male bird of the other pair, and none other than Tommy Dobbs,

with a new moustache looking like the business
end of an old tooth-brush, here lifted up his
voice with,—

"I say, Shanks! we are about to get up a
rowing-party to the island and back, and you
and Miss Mopus are booked to go."

"Oh, that will be nice!" said the young lady,
who was the one with whom Shanks was, as
Tommy said, rather coarsely, "keeping his
hand in." "Really, Mr. Sinclair, of all things
in the world a moonlight row is what I most
dote on."

And his name was Jack Sinclair. The girls
hereabout did not call him "Eyes," as did those
who knew him where he wore gray cloth and
pipe-clay; and yet they felt the magic of his
glance none the less.

In a few minutes the big barge, filled with a
jolly, melodious crowd, was off and away o'er
the waters blue, but Jack and Miss Mopus were
not in it.

How did this happen?

This was the way. When the party arrived
at the pier whence they were to descend into
the barge, Jack and Miss Mopus, who had
stopped to admire a cloud-effect or something

16

else, were a little in the rear of the column. I
say Jack *and* Miss Mopus, but it was Miss M.
who did the halting, and Jack, out of his
natural courtesy, forbore to urge her onward.
Poor boy! this gentleness cost him much.

So when they did at length reach the stairs at
the foot of which the barge rocked lazily, it—
the boat—was quite comfortably full, and the
only available place was a bit of a triangular
seat up in the bow, full of holes like a colan-
der, upon which Miss Mopus said she would *not*
sit: they must find room elsewhere.

"But, hang it!—I beg pardon!—you can't.
We're like a lot of sardines back here. Might
make room for *you*, Miss Mopus, and I'll give
way for Shanks and go ashore." All this from
Tommy Dobbs.

But Tommy's young lady was not going to
stand any such nonsense, and she said, in a low
but very energetic voice, that gave promise of
an uncertain future for him who should win—
I had almost said "and wear"—her; but *she*
would do the wearing,—

"Mr. Dobbs, you are not going to desert me
for *that* Mr. Shanks, I know."

Before Tommy could say a word either way

Shanks called out, in his big voice, "No, no, Chick! Stay where you are. There's a little 'dinky' tied somewhere here, and Miss Mopus and I will soon be in your wake. You will not mind going with me, Miss Mopus?"

"Oh, no; should be charmed, Mr. Shan— Mr. Sinclair."

So, as soon as the barge crew pulled away from the pier, Shanks, having found the "dinky," brought it to the foot of the dripping steps, and Miss Mopus was soon sitting in the stern-sheets, her hand on the tiller, having on the way thither made two ingeniously unsuccessful attempts to swamp the craft by twice convulsively seizing Shanks as he stood up to assist her across the thwarts. Off they went in the track of the bubbles left in the wake of the barge, now many yards ahead. But Shanks pulled a strong oar, and at first it looked as if the distance might decrease; but it didn't. The little boat was so light, and Miss Mopus was so— well, not heavy, but her heavenly body *was* of the first magnitude—that the "dinky's" bow stood up a little, and, as the light chopping sea slapped at her, showed just a little bit of keel. Consequently rowing was difficult work, even for one

who, like Shanks, had had the odor of brine in
his nostrils all his life. And thus it happened
that the barge, rapidly gaining, soon rounded the
rocky point of the island and was lost to view.

Shanks saw nothing of this, for, like the man
in the song, he "looked one way and rowed
another." Courtesy demanded that he should
look at his *vis-à-vis*, who *would* look at him and
talk, and he found it a pleasant thing to do,
though his heart was safe in the memory of the
one dear girl far away. Miss Mopus talked
very well; she was *very* pretty; and being like
Daisy in many things physical, there was, as I
have said, a certain tie, made up of interest, as
one would feel in gazing at a not-too-well-
drawn picture of a friend. Like and yet not
like. That sort of thing.

Well, the lady talked. They all do, bless
their dear souls!—yes. Some more than others,
—never less. And as she talked and gazed on
the handsome brown face before her, she paid
no attention to the course of the vessel she was
assumed to be steering, when, all at once,—
bump! and Miss Mopus fell nearly into the
arms of Shanks, who, easing oars, replaced the
lady, and remarked,—

"Great Scott! what's that?" And without waiting for a reply, turned his head to find that the nose of the "dinky" was fast in the sandy beach. So much for Miss Mopus's steering!

"I say, Miss Mopus, we can't cross the island, you know." And the youngster laughed.

It was not polite, and she chose to be in a little pet. One does not like to be told of one's faults, and least of all by the one who is dear, and Miss Mopus had begun to find that Shanks was very dear to her. There was enough in the situation—the moonlight, the everything—to make fire where but an hour ago was just a little smoke. And when Shanks apologized for his rudeness in his soothing way, Miss Mopus's heart fell fluttering at his feet. But he knew it not. Not he! He was too modest, too loyal to the girl whose blue lozenge, held by a golden thread about his neck, lay close against his heart (for he was a little bit sentimental), to dream that any one else could weave a tender thought for *him*. And yet when the Mopus laid her soft, white, perfectly modeled hand on his, pressing it just a little; looked with her deep gray eyes, that had a nice way of dilating and moistening, into his, and said in her full voice, so like Daisy's own, that she forgave him, it must be confessed that he felt a little queer. Man is called the sterner sex, but really, in a case of this kind, the odds are on the other side.

However, he said nothing,—nothing that his Daisy, had she then arisen like another Aphrodite from the sparkling foam, might not have listened to, but he did say,—

"The barge must be just round that point, and, if you like, Miss Mopus, we may as well scramble over the rocks and surprise them all. They won't expect to see us coming overland,—I know every step of the way."

"Nothing could be better, I'm sure, for I feel just a little cramped, from sitting so long. So good of you to propose a walk."

So Shanks sprang out, taking with him a light, three-pronged anchor secured by a line, the other end of which was reeved in a ring set in the bow. This he sunk in the sand, and then returned to the boat, from which he helped Miss Mopus to disembark, the seizing business being repeated as she skipped over the gunwale to the somewhat sloppy beach. Foreseeing that the ebbing tide might leave the boat high and dry, he gave it plenty of rope, and midway upon the line set a heavy stone to prevent the "slack" dragging the anchor. Then the pair started for the other side of the rocky point.

The way was rough and rugged, and the moon had a tantalizing way (Shanks thought,— Mopus didn't) of going behind bits of black with silver-edged cloud when they came to a place where the assistance of a strong arm was necessary. The situation was not without its charm, for when the moon chose to do the magic-lantern act, Miss Mopus would creep confidingly closer to her escort. Yet, notwithstanding the animal, man, usually becomes human under such circumstances, Shanks behaved in so stolid a way that Miss Mopus thought him decidedly the reverse. And so, in this manner, the pair surmounted the point and descended to the beach on its other side to find —nothing! No barge, no party, nothing but the beach glistening like a white ribbon twixt them and the deep, blue, moonlit expanse of dancing water that stretched away until it met the star-specked sky.

"Why—wh—where are they?" from Miss Mopus.

" They didn't land here at all," said Shanks, who had been looking up and down the smooth beach for tracks and footprints, but had found none.

" Then what shall we do ?"

" Only one thing to do,—go back."

And so they went back over the rocks with the same experience as to moon, clouds, and so on, but less enthusiasm on the part of Shanks, who didn't quite like the way the bargeites had given him the slip, as he thought. And he had let Miss Mopus steer! and, of course—but then it would be unmanly to blame *her.* He ought to have kept a sharp lookout and followed the barge. Miss Mopus was not at all put out. Hers was one of those large, unangular, indolent natures that seldom take things *au serieux* until they begin to look *very* black, and then—— But at present everything was roseate and fair in her mind's eye, and she may have clung a little closer to her escort's arm as they toiled up and down the smooth, moss-grown rocks that lay twixt them and the place where they had left the " dinky" dancing on the wave.

And when they got there, the " dinky" was— where ?

"We can't have lost our way! This, certainly, was the spot where we left our boat," said Shanks, dropping Miss Mopus's arm and running to the edge of the shore, apparently in search of something, which he soon found. It was a stone, beneath it a rope, the end of which was ragged, as if it had been sawed in twain. This was the end towards the sea. The other seemed to be fast; and going towards it, Shanks found the anchor as he had left it, half buried in the sand. It seemed that the ebb of the tide had tautened the line, and the swaying motion of the boat had caused the strands to part as they worked back and forth against the edges of the rough stone which Shanks had placed on it. This very precaution had caused the disaster.

With a sinking heart he turned to say what could not be left unsaid; but the lady did not wait for him. She was, to put it mildly, in a rage. She reasoned, or rather, she concluded, for in the state of mind she found herself in just then reason had no place, that poor Shanks had purposely kept out of the way of the larger boat, and that the disappearance of the "dinky" had been part of his plan. It was an outrageous thought, and she was insane enough to give it

words. She could have torn her tongue away
a moment afterwards when she saw the horror
that stood in his eyes.

For a moment Shanks was silent. Then he
spoke: "Miss Mopus, you wrong me terribly.
But it is not far to the Pool; I think I can
make it in an hour, and soon afterwards you
will be with your friends."

He slipped off the light sack he wore, and
kicking off his low shoes, ran swiftly to where
the sea met the shore. But she was at his side
in a moment, all anger gone, and, catching him
by the sleeve,—

"What do you mean to do?"

He stopped,—gently tried to take his arm
from her grasp, saying, quietly, "Swim to the
Pool, Miss Mopus. Do not detain me. The
tide is now at a stand, and time is precious."

"Swim! Oh, you will not be so rash! For
my sake, too, after I have been so—so—so unjust! To risk your like for——"

"Miss Mopus," said Shanks, "I *must* leave
you. I cannot permit——"

"You shall *not* go! That is, not without me;
I mean—— Oh! Jack, do you not understand what I mean? Forgive me for the horrid

words I spoke. What must you think of me!
Do not despise me, Jack; do not leave me!"
And with tears she threw her arms about him.

He endeavored to escape from the encircling
folds of her warm embrace, but so firm was her
convulsive clasp that without roughness he
could not. In vain he protested that he was
quite able to swim, that he had often accomplished even greater distances, and that she
ought for her own sake to release him and let
him take advantage of the tide ere it turned.
But to all this was she deaf, averring that she
would not cease to cling to him; that if he went
into the water it must be with her arms about
him; and at last, with beseeching tears and
frantic words, extorted from him a promise
which a moment later he cursed himself for
giving,—that he would abandon all thought of
swimming across the water, which now, owing
to the freshening breeze, was beginning to chop
about unpleasantly.

Then she let go, with a long sigh, and Shanks,
who saw that he was in for it, led her away
from the damp sand to where it was dryer and
less open to the moist and chilling wind. Then
he quickly brought together some of the flotsam

and jetsam that formed the high-water mark, and having in his pocket matches, made a fire. A large, hollowed rock formed a convenient resting-place, and soon Miss Mopus was, she said, quite comfortable. Shanks sat down on another rock near by, and, at Miss Mopus's desire, lit a cigar. She "adored cigars." But he was very silent. She thought to herself that, considering how affairs stood, he might say *something;* but she failed to take notice that the standing of these affairs was a little one-sided, and yet she was very happy. She might have been vexed at his moody silence had she not begun to be very sleepy. The long walk, the excitement and reaction, the fresh breeze, the warmth of the blazing pile, the fumes of the cigar, all combined to overcome her senses, and, leaning against the rock, she gently lapsed into the land of dreams.

Shanks sat still and pondered. He knew enough of the world to be certain that lots of unpleasant things would be said about them both, and as he smoked and thought, he resolved, as he glanced at the sleeping girl, that he would do all that any man might be called upon to do in such a case. Tender thoughts of Daisy came upon him, and the sweet tones of her voice as she had said good-by, after a week of bliss at Richfield, came back as if borne upon the wave. She would hear of this; he should certainly tell her of it. It would come best from him. Then came the thought: Why on earth those people over there did not send in search of them? Perhaps they were looking for them,—yet it was strange they did not come to the island. Then again, why should they come to the island? Altogether it was very unpleasant, and he longed for morning. At last the rosy sun shot up from the sea, and Shanks began to feel that, as the night had passed away, it might not prove such a confounded mess after all; so piling a few sticks on the dying embers, he lit a fresh cigar and strolled towards the beach.

When at the edge of the shore, he gazed anxiously towards the Pool, half expecting to see something setting their way; but no,—there was nothing. He looked back at the place where he had left his companion. She had not stirred. Then he walked along the beach, which soon bent seaward, when in the red light of the early sun he saw, close at hand, that which made his heart stop.

Not a hundred yards off, and held in a cluster of sharp, black rocks that stood up above the fast-rising wave, was a dark object that increasing daylight told him was a boat.

It was the " dinky." But how came it there? He saw it all: the ebbing tide had carried her that way,—she had jammed between the rocks, —the flood would soon carry her far away to sea. Not a moment was to be lost. In he plunged, and, after a few minutes' rough buffeting with the white-caps which boiled about the jagged cliffs, his hand was upon the gunwale of the boat, that with this slight shock floated free in an instant.

He lifted himself in; found the oars; at once, with a few swift nervous strokes, drove the " dinky" half her length upon the sandy beach, and a moment later stood dripping like a Triton before Miss Mopus, who at that instant awoke.

" How you startled me! Have I been asleep? But, Mr. Sinclair, why, are we—— Oh, yes, I remember now; and you are so wet,—it has not rained ?"

" Pardon me if I am abrupt. But we have not a moment to lose. The boat is waiting. Come !"

"The *boat!* And you have done what you said you would not do. You might have drowned, and what would have become of *me?* Oh, Mr.—Jack!"

"I have not been to the Pool, Miss Mopus," returned Shanks, who, in a few modest words, related what had happened. And then, in a moment more, the two castaways bade adieu to their island with light yet anxious hearts.

III.

WE have seen that the barge did not touch at the island, and hence it follows that, having circled it about, its crew took it back to the Pool, where the party were not a little surprised to learn that Shanks and Miss Mopus had not returned. Still, no one thought of danger, and, after a few rather loud whispers, the matter appeared to have been dismissed from the minds of all save Tommy and his fair enslaver.

"Hang it! you know," said little Tommy, "I don't like it at all. Engaged, you know, to the very loveliest creature you ever saw,"—a doubtful sniff from the lady,—"and to go off and *stay off* in this way with *another girl!* It's not a bit like old Shanks, Miss Bang,—well, Ophelia, then."

"As for your Miss Mopus——"

"*My* Miss Mopus! Well, I like that. Really, Miss Ban—Ophelia, then——"

"Be good enough not to interrupt. I am not surprised at any extraordinary departure from—from—well, you know what I mean—on the part of that young person; and as for *that* Mr. Shanks,—as he calls himself,—well, all men are alike."

"I say, you know, Miss Ba—Ophelia, then, if all men *were* like old Shanks, what a jolly world this would be! Eh!"

Miss Bang might have retorted, but she refrained; and the bright promise of an affectionate "good-night" was eclipsed by the appearance on the scene of Mr. and Mrs. Mopus, who were naturally worried about their daughter. So the vestal Bang withdrew, accompanied by the small, malodorous watering-place lamp, leaving her Thomas to confront the anxious parents.

To them Tommy told all that he knew, and wound up by advising them to go to bed, saying that everything was sure to be right, and that

he would go down to the pier and wait for the
truants. He confessed to himself that he did
not see what good this would do, nor why it
should have any soothing effect; but the old
people appeared to be easier, and that was
something.

When the "dinky" hove in sight the next
morning, an hour after sunrise, Tommy, with a
severe face, stood at the head of the steps.

He bowed with grave courtesy to Miss Mopus
as she came up leaning on Shanks's arm, and
seemed half annoyed that she met his gaze so
frankly. She put him wonderfully in mind of
the Daisy as she had appeared upon her return
to the ball-room that moonlit eve in June *minus*
the blue button, and he couldn't understand it
at all. Shanks was very damp and *distrait*, and
though he bore himself not untenderly towards
his companion, there was nothing in his appearance to recall the night when he had lost a
button. Tommy was not sorry to see his friend
thus, but he did not like to find him quite so
haggard and constrained.

"Hang it!" he said to himself, "I don't like
it!"

As soon as they reached the hotel, Miss

17*

Mopus flew to her mamma, where, if you please, we will leave her for the present.

"Now!" said Tommy, "come to my room. I want to talk with you. Come!" The little man's dignity and abruptness would, under other circumstances, have brought a laugh from Shanks, but he felt the premonitory chill that heralds coming clouds, and meekly followed Tommy to No. 44. His own was No. 45; the two communicated. The little chap offered him a wicker flask, saying, "I brought that from home." And while Shanks helped himself, went on,—

"Do you know what you have been about?"

"Do I know? Of course I know that I've got that girl into a pretty mess,—and myself, too. But, Chick, it was all a mistake——"

"Do you call it a 'mistake' to stay out all night with——"

"Stop! not another word until you have heard me!" And then he rapidly told the story of the night's adventure.

Before he had finished, Tommy's left arm was about his shoulders and their right hands were clasped.

"But," said Tommy, "my dear fellow, you

must not hope that this will go down with the hollow crowd. If you *hadn't* found your boat and had stayed on the island until some of the natives had picked you up, it would have been better,—romantic, you know, and all that. But, from your own view of the case, I ask you what sort of a story will that woman from the Pacific slope, Mrs. Rummill, and her shadow, Miss Ekko, create out of such materials? What can you do? Then there's poor Miss Mopus. Fight? yes; but you can't call out the world. And as for the fair sex,—you know the luck Don Quixote had with the windmills."

"Well, then, what *am* I to do?"

"Blessed if I know! Yes: take off those wet things and go to bed. I will be on the *qui vive* for public opinion, and—there goes the gong: I'm off!"

So Shanks turned in, and Tommy went to breakfast.

When Tommy returned to where he had left Shanks, one end of the matutinal cigar had gone out, while that which he held between his teeth was much out of condition. He was in such a rage. He slammed the door, flung his dumpy carcass into a chair, kicked the table, swore a little; and this awoke Shanks, lying in the next room, who called out,—

"That you, Chick? What's the matter?"

"No end of a row. I shall not be surprised if you have a visit from Papa Mopus; so you had better get up and——"

"What the devil—— You don't really mean——"

"Yes, I do. That poor girl came down to breakfast with mamma just as if everything was all right, and——"

"Well, isn't it?"

"Wait till I tell you. You need not fly out at *me*."

"Pardon, old fellow. *Go* on."

"Granted. Now be quiet. As I was saying, Miss Mopus came down fresh, smiling, and looking as happy as if—— I'm afraid you've made a mash there, Shanks."

"Stuff!"

"Well, I was about to say 'sour mash,' of course, knowing how you stand in—in—another quarter; but every confounded woman in the place turned her back upon her. Cold cut and no mistake. And then they began to talk at her in that nice way women have. Said all sorts of really brutal things about you two being out all night, and that sort of thing. She couldn't help hearing,—they didn't whisper,—and after sitting a few moments at table, looking, as each horrid speech fell upon her ear, as if she had been stabbed, she burst into tears and rushed out of the room."

"Great heaven! what have I done?" from Shanks, now dressed and walking up and down Tommy's apartment.

"You? nothing! Couldn't be helped, of course. And yet——" A mute shrug of the shoulders from Tommy, who then went on: "I couldn't stand this, you know, and broke out in a way that forced people to listen, and told the whole story."

"Thanks! thanks!"

"Well, the men—there were not many about—seemed to see how it was; but the women—even my Ophe—Miss Bang, I mean—were worse than before. That horrid one—all red satin and diamonds—sneered out, 'Quite the Romance of a Poor Young Man,' and Miss Ekko, of course, came in with 'Poor Young Man.'"

Shanks, with something between a curse and a groan, dropped into a chair.

Tommy continued: "Then I went out. I felt that if I didn't go away I might say something. So I went off to the beach; but whom should I run across there but that fellow Swag, —J. B. Swag he calls himself. He was disposed to be confidential, but I promptly intimated to him that if he had any remarks to make it would give me pleasure to name a friend, who would make the usual arrangements. I don't think he knew quite what I meant; but, if he had been a Kentucky gentleman instead of a J. B. Swag——"

A knock at the door, which being opened disclosed a servant, who bore the card of Papa Mopus, upon which was a penciled request for a few moments' private conversation with Lieutenant Sinclair.

"Show him up," said Tommy; and as the door closed, "Let him come in here, old chap. I'll get out for a bit." And, taking his friend's hand, he added: "Keep up your end of the log; it's all right, you know."

"Never fear," returned Shanks; "I'll face the music."

The twins shook hands. Tommy descended to the parlors, and soon afterwards did penance

by "holding" worsted for Miss Bang, who was
engaged upon a thing *she* called an afghan.
Some called it Penelope's web.

The interview between Mr. Mopus and
Shanks was said by those ladies whose rooms
were on the same floor to have been "very
quiet." They omitted to explain how they
knew this, but they "knew" such a lot of
things, that the Mopus family found it convenient and merciful for themselves to leave the
Pool that same day.

The beach that afternoon was the scene of
another interview, one which afforded entertain-
ment and occupation for many eyes and tongues.
The twins were in earnest conversation, frequently halting as if to emphasize their remarks, and it was observed that Shanks appeared to be resolved upon something which
seemed to call forth much energetic remonstrance from Tommy. Miss Bang, who, like
the rest, could not hear a word, was, in consequence, fairly bubbling with that kind of
wrath which seems to boil best 'neath vestal
flame, and alluded to the now absent Miss
Mopus as a "creature."

The gong sounded as the pair approached the

house. Shanks went to his room,—didn't want any tea; but Tommy, whose appetite was proof against everything but repletion, took his charmer in to table, where he nearly choked with rage and cold beef while the red satin female from the Pacific slope, her Miss Ekko, and his Ophelia made mincemeat of the departed Miss Mopus.

Next morning when the little man arose, he found upon his table a letter from Shanks, containing another, and explaining that he had gone,—didn't care to say good-by,—would soon meet him at Fort ——, their station, and would he, when in New York, deliver the inclosed?

Poor Tommy burst out crying. "He's done it, then! He said he would. Poor, dear boy! What an ass! Confound those women!"

IV.

It was September, in New York. The Van Stumps had returned. Mr. Van Stump was in stocks,—couldn't stay away any longer; his rosy spouse declared there was nothing to eat in the country,—she was nearly starved; and Daisy was eager to see "Eyes,"—he would be in the city in September.

She had not had a letter for a week; but he was at the seaside,—yachting, perhaps; he would come himself, soon. Every ring at the door-bell made her heart throb; but he came not.

One morning while at breakfast she saw in the *Herald* something that nearly stunned her. She looked again, doubting the evidence of her own eyes, to see announced the marriage of Lieutenant John Sinclair, U. S. Army, to Isabella, daughter of Mark Mopus, of ——. She could read no more, but sat like a stone for a time, then rose and left the table, taking the newspaper with her to her own room. There, she locked the door, and tried to think. It was all over, then. Her dream had vanished; she had thought herself so happy, and now—— But, stay,—it might not be *her* John Sinclair after all: it might be a trick,—a hoax. She had heard such things talked about. But then came the doubt, why had he not written? Why this? Why that? It seemed to her that until she *knew* that he had been false she must have faith in him.

A ring at the door-bell!

It caused her heart to throb, but it was not

the eager, expectant leap of yesterday. It was that of dread.

A knock on her door. A card:

> " Lieutenant Thomas Dobbs,
>   *U.S.A.*"

It was not "Eyes;" but it was his dear friend.

She might learn from him. Yes, she would see him at once. And down the stairs, with the fatal newspaper in her hand, she slowly walked to meet poor little Tommy, who would have looked only less like a wraith than herself if he could have looked like a wraith at all.

Without waiting to offer any conventional remarks, Tommy, pointing to the paper she carried, said,—

"You have seen it, then? This, perhaps" (here he presented the letter Shanks had confided to him), "will tell you all. I can't." And the tears stood in the little fellow's round, honest eyes and trembled in his voice.

She took it, but did not then break the seal.

"'This will tell me all.' All? What? Nay, do not speak, Mr. Dobbs; I will read the letter."

She was very calm, although one hand played

in a fitful way with a bell-button that hung from a chatelaine she wore.

"Yes; read it, and let me say—you know—good-by. I *couldn't* see you read it" (the tears were chasing one another down his cheeks). "And so, Miss—Miss—Daisy,—*he* always called you that,—I'll say—goo—good-by."

They shook hands and parted.

Tommy went to his hotel, rushed to his room, and passed the day in a most miserable state, forgetting all about dinner and Miss Bang,—the last-named charmer having returned to town.

She went to *her* room. There she broke the seal and read "Eyes's" truthful account of what had occurred at the Pool. His letter concluded with this:

"And now, my heart's own darling,—let me call you so for the last time,—I shall never call any one else so dearly,—you know what I *must* do. Such terrible things have been said—you, dear, sweet, pure heart, can never guess what—about this poor girl, that I, knowing myself to be their cause, feel that there is but one thing left for me to do. God forgive me if it be wrong. But I feel that it will be only right. I shall keep the blue button, dear, unless you

send mine back to me. We shall meet again
some day, but not here. God bless you, and
farewell!"

Later, those who sought her found her lying
in a faint upon the floor.

*   *   *   *   *   *

Among those who rode into the Valley of the
Shadow of Death, which, one bright morning
in June, lay crouching in swart, abhorrent form,
was no better soldier than Lieutenant John Sinclair, of the —th Cavalry, who, during the short
halt which preceded the subsequent attack,
crossed over to where little Tommy Dobbs, on a
large and sedate horse, sat wondering what they
were going to do next.

"Chick, old fellow," said Shanks, in his
gentle way,—gentler now than of yore,—
"Chick, good-by!" And he held out his hand,
which Tommy squeezed.

"Eh? Oh, of course. Good-by, Shanks.
What's up now?"

"Simply, Tommy, that I don't think I shall
get out of this affair. There's going to be hot
work."

"Oh, come now, old fellow! You mustn't
talk about not pulling through. It won't be

much of a row. These things never are, you
know. Blaze away all day; great waste of
ammunition; Indians suddenly disappear; long
accounts from 'Our Special Correspondent;'
everybody's trousers worn out, and nobody
hurt. That's the style."

"Yes, I know; but this will be different, and
I want you to take charge of this and return it
to—— You know, Chick." And he made as
if he would take something from within the
breast of the blue hunting-shirt he had on
beneath his blouse. But at this moment the
word was passed to mount, and Tommy, who
was a little way off from his troop, dug spurs
into his staid beast and cantered away, calling
out,—

"Can't stop now, Shanks. It's all right.
See you to-night. Dine with us,—antelope and
slapjacks!"

And when the smoke had cleared away,
among the mutilated, despoiled, and slain were
said to be Shanks Sinclair and Chiquito Dobbs,
but their corpses could not be recognized.

And when Rain-in-the-Face rode insolently
into the agency at ——, on the Upper Missouri,
the wind that stirred the lappels of the cavalry

officer's blouse he wore (bloody, torn, and stained) exposed upon his tawny breast a blue satin button.

Above a little iron cot within a cloistered room hangs a wreath of faded immortelles, within which in withered violets are the letters " J. S.," and from the wreath depends one silver button.

THE END.

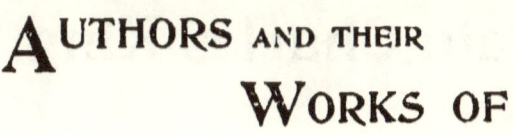

AUTHORS AND THEIR
WORKS OF
Fiction.

Selected from the Catalogue of

J. B. LIPPINCOTT COMPANY.

COMPLETE CATALOGUE SENT
UPON APPLICATION.

Captain Charles King, U.S.A.

Under Fire. *Illustrated. Cloth, $1.25.*

The Colonel's Daughter. *Illustrated. Cloth, $1.25.*

Marian's Faith. *Illustrated. Cloth, $1.25.*

Captain Blake. *Illustrated. Cloth, $1.25.*

Foes in Ambush. *Cloth, $1.25.*

Kitty's Conquest. *Cloth, $1.00.*

Starlight Ranch, and Other Stories. *Cloth, $1.00.*

Laramie; or, The Queen of Bedlam. *Cloth, $1.00.*

The Deserter, and From the Ranks. *Cloth, $1.00.*

Two Soldiers, and Dunraven Ranch. *Cloth, $1.00.*

A Soldier's Secret, and An Army Portia. *Cloth, $1.00.*

Waring's Peril. *Cloth, $1.00.*

EDITOR OF

The Colonel's Christmas Dinner, and Other Stories. *Cloth, $1.25.*

An Initial Experience, and Other Stories. *Cloth, $1.00.*

"From the lowest soldier to the highest officer, from the servant to the master, there is not a character in any of Captain King's novels that is not wholly in keeping with expressed sentiments. There is not a movement made on the field, not a break from the ranks, not an offence against the military code of discipline, and hardly a heart-beat that escapes his watchfulness."—*Boston Herald.*

J. B. Lippincott Company, Philadelphia.

"THE DUCHESS."

Peter's Wife.

Lady Patty.   A Little Irish Girl.

The Hoyden.

12mo. Paper, 50 cents; cloth, $1.00.

Phyllis.	Mrs. Geoffrey.
Molly Bawn.	Portia.
Airy Fairy Lilian.	Löys, Lord Berresford, and
Beauty's Daughters.	other Stories.
Faith and Unfaith.	Rossmoyne.
Doris.	A Mental Struggle.
"O Tender Dolores."	Lady Valworth's Diamonds.
A Maiden All Forlorn.	Lady Branksmere.
In Durance Vile.	A Modern Circe.
The Duchess.	The Honourable Mrs. Vere-
Marvel.	ker.
Jerry, and other Stories.	Under-Currents.

A Life's Remorse.

Bound only in Cloth, $1.00.

"'The Duchess' has well deserved the title of being one of the most fascinating novelists of the day. The stories written by her are the airiest, lightest, and brightest imaginable; full of wit, spirit, and gayety, yet containing touches of the most exquisite pathos. There is something good in all of them."—*London Academy.*

J. B. Lippincott Company, Philadelphia.

Mrs. H. Lovett Cameron.

A Tragic Blunder.

A Daughter's Heart.   **A Sister's Sin.**

Jack's Secret.

12mo.   Paper, 50 cents ; cloth, $1.00.

"Mrs. Cameron's novels, 'In a Grass Country,' 'A Daughter's Heart,' 'A Sister's Sin,' 'Jack's Secret,' have shown a high skill in inventing interesting plots and delineating character. All her stories are vivid in action and pure in tone. This one, 'A Tragic Blunder,' is equal to her best."—*National Tribune.*

This Wicked World.

In a Grass Country.   **A Devout Lover.**

Vera Neville.   **A Life's Mistake.**

Pure Gold.   **Worth Winning.**

The Cost of a Lie.   **A Lost Wife.**

Cloth, $1.00.

"The works of this author are always pure in character, and can be safely put into the hands of young as well as old."—*Norristown Herald.*

"A wide circle of admirers always welcome a new work by this favorite author. Her style is pure and interesting, and she depicts marvellously well the daily social life of the English people."—*St. Louis Republic.*

J. B. Lippincott Company, Philadelphia.

OUIDA.

Two Offenders.

12mo. Cloth, $1.00.

Syrlin.   **Guilderoy.**

12mo. Paper, 50 cents; cloth, $1.00.

Othmar.	In a Winter City.
A House-Party.	Ariadne.
Puck.	Friendship.
Pascarel.	Moths.
Bébée.	Beatrice Boville.
Signa.	Chandos.
Cecil Castlemaine's Gage.	Tricotrin.
Folle-Farine.	Under Two Flags.
Granville de Vigne.	A Village Commune.
Idalia.	In Maremma.
Randolph Gordon.	Princess Napraxine.
Strathmore.	Wanda.

12mo. Cloth, $1.00; paper, 40 cents.

"Ouida is one of the most interesting writers of her time. She has close observation, much imaginative fertility, a copious vocabulary, and a retentive memory."—*New York Herald.*

"Ouida's stories are abundant in world-knowledge and world-wisdom, strong and interesting in plot. Her characters are conceived and elaborated with a skill little short of masterly, and the reflective portions of her stories are marked by fine thought and a deep insight into the workings of human nature."—*Boston Gazette.*

J. B. Lippincott Company, Philadelphia.

MRS. A. L. WISTER.

Translations from the German.

$1.00 per volume.

Countess Erika's Apprenticeship. By Ossip Schubin.

"O Thou, My Austria!" By Ossip Schubin.

Erlach Court. By Ossip Schubin.

The Alpine Fay. By E. Werner.

The Owl's Nest. By E. Marlitt.

Picked Up in the Streets. By H. Schobert.

Saint Michael. By E. Werner.

Violetta. By Ursula Zoge von Manteufel.

The Lady with the Rubies. By E. Marlitt.

Vain Forebodings. By E. Oswald.

A Penniless Girl. By W. Heimburg.

Quicksands. By Adolph Streckfuss.

Countess Gisela. By E. Marlitt.

At the Councillor's. By E. Marlitt.

The Second Wife. By E. Marlitt.

The Old Mam'selle's Secret. By E. Marlitt.

Gold Elsie. By E. Marlitt.

The Little Moorland Princess. By E. Marlitt.

Banned and Blessed. By E. Werner.

A Noble Name. By Claire von Glümer.

MRS. WISTER'S TRANSLATIONS.

Continued.

From Hand to Hand. By Golo Raimund.

Severa. By E. Hartner.

A New Race. By Golo Raimund.

The Eichhofs. By Moritz von Reichenbach.

Castle Hohenwald. By Adolph Streckfuss.

Margarethe. By E. Juncker.

Too Rich. By Adolph Streckfuss.

A Family Feud. By Ludwig Harder.

The Green Gate. By Ernst Wichert.

Only a Girl. By Wilhelmine von Hillern.

Why Did He Not Die. By Ad. von Volckhauser.

Hulda. By Fanny Lewald.

The Bailiff's Maid. By E. Marlitt.

In the Schillingscourt. By E. Marlitt.

"Mrs. A. L. Wister, through her many translations of novels from the German, has established a reputation of the highest order for literary judgment, and for a long time her name upon the title-page of such a translation has been a sufficient guarantee to the lovers of fiction of a pure and elevating character, that the novel would be a cherished home favorite. This faith in Mrs. Wister is fully justified by the fact that among her more than thirty translations that have been published by Lippincott's there has not been a single disappointment. And to the exquisite judgment of selection is to be added the rare excellence of her translations, which has commanded the admiration of literary and linguistic scholars." —*Boston Home Journal.*

J. B. Lippincott Company, Philadelphia.

HANDLEY CROSS
SPORTING NOVELS.

"Jorrocks" Edition.

Handley Cross; or, Mr. Jorrock's Hunt.

Ask Mamma; or, The Richest Commoner in England.

Mr. Facey Romford's Hounds.

Sponge's Sporting Tour.

Plain or Ringlets?

Hawbuck Grange; or, The Sporting Adventures of Thomas Scott, Esq.

In six 8vo volumes, with numerous illustrations,
$2.25 per vol.

"This inimitable series of volumes is absolutely unique, there being nothing approaching to them in all the wide range of modern or ancient literature. Written by Mr. Surtees, a well-known country gentleman, who was passionately devoted to the healthy sport of fox-hunting, and gifted with a keen spirit of manly humor of a Rabelaisian tinge, they abound with incidents redolent of mirth and jollity. The artist, Mr. Leech, was himself also an enthusiast in the sport, and has reflected in his illustrations, with instinctive appreciation, the rollicking abandon of the author's stories.

J. B. Lippincott Company, Philadelphia.

JULIEN GORDON.

"Now and then, to prove to men—perhaps also to prove to themselves—what they can do if they dare and will, one of these gifted women detaches herself from her sisters, enters the arena with men, to fight for the highest prizes, and as the brave Gotz says of Brother Martin, 'shames many a knight.' To this race of conquerors belongs to-day one of the first living writers of novels and romances, Julien Gordon."

FRIEDRICH SPIELHAGEN.

Poppæa.

A Diplomat's Diary.

A Successful Man.

Vampires, and Mademoiselle Réséda.

Two stories in one book.

12mo. Cloth, $1.00 per vol.

"The cleverness and lightness of touch which characterized 'A Diplomat's Diary' are not wanting in the later work of the American lady who writes under the pseudonyme of Julien Gordon. In her former story the dialogue is pointed and alert, the characters are clear-cut and distinct, and the descriptions picturesque. As for the main idea of 'A Successful Man,' the intersection of two wholly different strata of American life,—one fast and fashionable, the other domestic and decorous,—it is worked out with much skill and alertness of treatment to its inevitably tragic issue."—*N. Y. World.*

J. B. Lippincott Company, Philadelphia.

Mrs. George McClellan.

(HARFORD FLEMMING.)

Broken Chords.

12mo. Paper, 50 cents; cloth, $1.25.

"The story is developed with so subtle a skill that it is difficult to give an adequate resume of it in a brief space. It is sufficient to say, however, that it will arrest the attention of the two most numerous classes of readers,—the fiction-loving and the ethical." —*Boston Advertiser.*

Broken Chords.
Cupid and the Sphinx.
A Carpet Knight.

12mo. Cloth, gilt top, three volumes in neat box, $3.00.

"In response to a persistent demand for the novels of Mrs. George McClellan ('Harford Flemming'), it has been decided to republish her works in a library edition, bound in an attractive uniform of dark blue, with decoration of white panelling. 'Cupid and the Sphinx,' a charming novel of life in Egypt, was first suggested by a statue which Mrs. McClellan observed in Mr. Story's studio at Rome. Mrs. McClellan comes of a gifted family, and her habit of careful observation and exact description is as evident in the control of her characters and plot as in the purely descriptive passages.

"These traits reappear in 'The Carpet Knight,' a Philadelphia society story displaying clever delineation of types and keen analysis of character, and in 'Broken Chords,' a glimpse of real life and tenderly human romance."—*Philadelphia Ledger.*

J. B. Lippincott Company, Philadelphia.

AMÉLIE RIVES.

The Quick or the Dead?

12mo. Cloth, $1.00.

"To me her novels are of the greatest interest and value : they have suggested new trains of thought ; given me new ideas ; opened up new vistas—in fact, their reading has been not only pleasurable, but profitable."—*New York Herald.*

The Witness of the Sun.

12mo. Paper, 50 cents ; cloth, $1.00.

"The wide discussion created by Miss Rives's 'Quick or the Dead?' has caused a great demand for her new work, which, in several respects, is superior to her first novel. The dramatic situations are stronger, the characters are more carefully drawn, and there is less luxuriousness of expression."—*Norristown Herald.*

Barbara Dering.

A Sequel to "The Quick or the Dead?" 12mo. Paper, 50 cents ; cloth, $1.25.

"Many of the people who objected to the character of her work before will object again ; but, on the other hand, many men and women will be deeply impressed by the new story, will own to themselves, if not to others, that she has spoken the truth, that her characters are true to life ; will agree with her conclusions, and some will thank her for having done a good deed. The book is brilliantly written from the stand-point of a young woman of observation, experience, feeling, and strong convictions, and will 'strike home' in the hearts of many readers."—*St. Paul Dispatch.*

J. B. Lippincott Company, Philadelphia.

JOHN STRANGE WINTER

(MRS. ARTHUR STANNARD.)

Every Inch a Soldier.

12mo. Paper, 50 cents; cloth, $1.00.

"Of the incidents of the work before us, the plot is highly entertaining, and incidentally we meet the Bishop of Blankhampton, whose matrimonial affairs were ably discussed in a book previously written. It is a very pleasant and readable book, and we are glad to see it."—*Norristown Herald.*

Aunt Johnnie.

12mo. Paper, 50 cents; cloth, $1.00.

"Mrs. Stannard preserves her freshness and vivacity in a wonderful way. 'Aunt Johnnie' is as bright and amusing a story as any that she has written, and it rattles on from the first chapter to the last with unabated gayety and vigor. The hero and heroine are both charming, and the frisky matron who gives the story its name is a capitally managed character. The novel is exactly suited to the season, and is sure to be very popular."—*Charleston News and Courier.*

The Other Man's Wife.

12mo. Paper, 50 cents; cloth, $1.00.

"The hero and heroine have a charm which is really unusual in these hackneyed personages, for they are most attractive and wholesome types. Indeed, wholesomeness may be said to be the most notable characteristic of this author's work."—*N. Y. Telegram.*

Only Human.

12mo. Paper, 50 cents; cloth, $1.00.

"A bright and interesting story. . . . Its pathos and humor are of the same admirable quality that is found in all the other novels by this author."—*Boston Gazette.*

J. B. Lippincott Company, Philadelphia.

MARIE CORELLI.

Barabbas.

A Dream of the World's Tragedy.

12mo. Cloth, $1.00.

"A book which aroused in some quarters more violent hostility than any book of recent years. By most secular critics the authoress was accused of bad taste, bad art, and gross blasphemy; but, in curious contrast, most of the religious papers acknowledged the reverence of treatment and the dignity of conception which characterized the work."—*London Athenæum.*

"It is a remarkable story in many ways, bold yet reverent in its handling of the great and solemn facts of the trial, crucifixion, and resurrection of Jesus, striking in its fresh and sympathetic representations of Judas, Barabbas, and others, uplifting in its tender and beautiful conception of Christ, and brilliant in its descriptions."—*Boston Congregationalist.*

Vendetta;

Or, The Story of One Forgotten.

12mo. Cloth, $1.00.

"It is a thrilling and irresistibly charming book."—*Baltimore American.*

"The story is Italian, the time 1884, and the precise stage of the acts, Naples, during the last visitation of the cholera. A romance, but a romance of reality. No mind of man can imagine incidents so wonderful, so amazing as those of actual occurrence. While the story is exciting, and must be read through when once begun, it furnishes a vivid and impressive picture of Italian life and morals."—*Washington National Republican.*

J. B. Lippincott Company, Philadelphia.

MY PARIS NOTE=BOOK.

12mo. Cloth, $1.25.

"Victor Emanuel, the members of the Comédie Française, Ernest Renan, Paul de Kock, MacMahon, Thiers, Grévy and his wife, Ferry, Freycinet, Boulanger and Mme. de Bonnemain, Skobeleff, Clémenceau, Gambetta, Brisson, Goblet, Floquet, Cassagnac, surely these are names to conjure with, and it is of these notables that Mr. Vandam tells us at length in his spicy, gossipy style. Verily his note-book is a mine of wealth, and all will hope that he will open it once more and many times."—*Cincinnati Tribune.*

"The author of that much-talked-of book, 'An Englishman in Paris,' has written another, which will create as great an interest as the first. The book is a fund of enjoyment from beginning to end, and any one who takes it up will find himself interested."—*Boston Times.*

"This new volume by the author of 'An Englishman in Paris,' is one of the most readable of the books of the year. It abounds in the brightest of sketches, in the most interesting of gossip, in the most vivid of descriptions of the altogether unique Paris under the third republic."—*Boston Daily Advertiser.*

"The book, which comes to us from the Lippincotts, is fully as entertaining as its predecessor, and is quite as rich in illustrative anecdotes of eminent men and important events. We are again brought into intimate relations with Louis Napoleon ; we are taken behind the scenes of the Comédie Française ; we make the acquaintance of Renan, Paul de Kock, Thiers, Jules Grévy,—in a word, the most interesting phases of recent and contemporary French life are exposed to us by one who has known the boulevards for almost forty years, and who has had, besides, the use of certain valuable reminiscences recorded by two maternal granduncles, who lived on terms of intimacy with Napoleon III."—*Philadelphia Press.*

J. B. Lippincott Company, Philadelphia.